THE

DEADLY SINS
7

COMPILED BY
THE NEFARIOUS AND THE DAMNED
DIANE NARRAWAY & MARISHA KIDDLE

All rights reserved, no part of this publication may be reproduced or transmitted by any means whatsoever without the prior permission of the publisher or artists.

Edited by Veneficia Publications
Additional editing by Fi Woods
Cover image by Kayla Mavrakis
All other images by Alex Cassford

ISBN: 979-8-856076-82-9

Veneficia Publications
July 2023

VENEFICIA PUBLICATIONS UK
veneficiapublications.com

This is the world of the sinner—
enter at your own risk ...

CONTENTS

THE DEADLY SEVEN – DIANE NARRAWAY   i

ENVY

ENVY – DIANE NARRAWAY	2
DAMNATION – ALEX CASSFORD	3
RIDDLE OF THE OLDEST ADVERSARY – JUDI MOORE	6
THE GREEN-EYED MONSTER – FI WOODS	7
MEI LIN – DIANE NARRAWAY	15

GLUTTONY

GLUTTONY – DIANE NARRAWAY	21
THE CONFESSION OF SAMUEL KEEPS – KATE KNIGHT	22
XMAS 1989 – JUDI MOORE	31

GREED

| GREED – DIANE NARRAWAY | 34 |
| OWN GOAL – G.W. HAWKER | 35 |

LUST

LUST – SCARLETT PAIGE	47
DOLLY LANE – DIANE NARRAWAY	49
MY SWEET DOLLY LANE – DIANE NARRAWAY	65
LUST TO DUST – BEKKI MILNER	67
THE QUEEN AND THE JAILOR – DEFOE SMITH	69
THE REAL BOY – SCARLETT PAIGE	76

PRIDE

| PRIDE – DIANE NARRAWAY | 87 |
| THE SWAN SONG OF TWO SISTERS – JENNIE JONES | 88 |

SIN AND BONE – KATHY SHARP	105
COWBOY PIE – FI WOODS	108
THE IRIZINIUM PRIESTESS – MOIRA HODGKINSON	118
THE TALE OF MARY DEVLIN – GERALDINE LAMBERT	128

SLOTH

SLOTH – DIANE NARRAWAY	146
NOT GUILTY – MARISHA KIDDLE	148
BELPHEGOR – BEKKI MILNER	152

WRATH

WRATH – SCARLETT PAIGE	164
THE WRATH OF ANN FIELDS – KATE KNIGHT	166
THE HAND OF WRATH – SCOTT IRVINE	172
WILLIAM – KATE KNIGHT	188

HERE THERE BE DRAGONS – AN OUTRO BY DEFOE SMITH

THE DEADLY SEVEN
Diane Narraway

The pain is indescribable; the unrelenting pain, the agonising gnawing constantly eating away at my very soul. It is beyond just wanting her sexually. Lust?

Well, now that would be easy to deal with. I don't just want to sleep with her, I want her completely. I want to be the one she wakes up with, the one she shares her morning coffee and toast with. I want to pick her up when she falls, and I long to share her hopes and dreams. I want to be the one, her one and only, just as she is mine. Quite simply I want to be you.

I remember the first time I saw her, at the petrol station. I wanted her, desperately wanted her. She didn't notice, but you did, didn't you? Was it that obvious? I suppose it must have been, because I remember the anger on your face as you watched me lust after your wife. She was oblivious to anyone but you. That's what hurts the most: that she doesn't even see me; she never sees anything but you. Over the past few months, I have felt my moment of lust grow into envy and anger, until it is hard to see where one ends and the other begins.

It doesn't stop there, because my anger turns to rage as I seek to satiate my unyielding desire. I have gorged on wine and overindulged on the finest foods. My love, for make no mistake, although my love is obsessive, it is still love fuelled by a darker passion, a burning desire to own. My need to satisfy my overwhelming hunger drives me to excess and, in turn, my gluttony slows my body and I languish malcontentedly.

I become obsessed with work, but you and I both know it is not the money I desire; yet in the absence of all that I truly crave, greed becomes my master. It is not enough—it is never enough, and it never will be, as long as she is with you and not me, and my pride.

Yes, somewhere, deep inside, I still have some pride. You may smile but it will be me who has the last laugh, because with you gone she will be free, and I will be there to console her, free to love her and to be loved by her. Is that a tear I see roll down your face? Of course, it is. I would be tearful too if I was in your position. Still, it won't be long now. Do you have any last words? No? OK.

As I watch the blood pour from my rival's body I feel relief, and perhaps a tinge of sorrow at his loss, but mostly relief. I casually glance out of the window and notice her entering the café over the road. Suddenly I am gripped with terror. The fear is overwhelming and then my fears are realised: she is meeting a man. I watch her kiss him.

How can she? After all that I've been through. I look down at her husband tied up and dead on my kitchen chair, and for the first time, I notice the letter sticking out of his pocket. I grab it and, through blurred eyes, I read the words, 'Decree Nisi.'

ENVY

ENVY
Diane Narraway

Your obsessive yearning
For your heart's desire
Consumes all you are,
And burns like fire.
It seeps into every cell and more:
Devouring all the good,
Leaving you rotten to the core.
Yet still you covet thy neighbour's wife,
And when all is done and said,
That green-eyed monster's eyes.
Glow a darker shade of red.
Just how far will you go,
To get all you think you need?
What rules that voice within?
What demon plants the seed?
What rules your heart,
And brings confusion to your mind?
That old devil—jealousy—
Both treacherous, and unkind.

DAMNATION
Alex Cassford

Messy,
Chaotic,
Selfish,
Unfair.
That is what this world was—it was **Unfair.**

And the people within this world are **Undeserving** ... but they got it all ... everything that I **Wanted;** everything I **Deserved.** They had it and all they did was flaunt it, and highlight everything that I was **Lacking:**

Money,
Power,
Fame,
Family,
Friends,
Love,
Happiness ...

All of it. All of it was so **Unfair.**

To rub salt into my wounds, they were all so **Oblivious.** They had eyes but were completely blind to the poison that seeped through the chinks in my fleshy armour, infiltrating the life blood winding through those crimson trenches, slowly plaguing my mind, my heart, and my soul. It was their **Contentment** that blinded them, serving as rose-tinted glasses that protected them from the disease that festered within me, feeding my insecurities, the darker thoughts that I was once blissfully ignorant of.

I wanted it. I wanted everything that they had—everything that I lacked:

Their **Money,**
Their **Power,**
Their **Fame,**
Their **Family,**
Their **Friends,**
Their **Love,**
Their **Happiness** ...

Didn't I at least deserve their **Contentment?**

All of it. All of it was so **Unfair.**

They were **Undeserving** of their shackleless lives; free from the tight coils that bound me to the bitterness brewing behind the fleshy walls of my fabricated fortress. It was **Unfair** how they got to fly so freely, so **Recklessly,** whilst my once white-feathered wings, deceived me with empty promises of flight and freedom, burning and melting as I flew higher and higher, consuming me with the sweet fragrances of all I could have had.

As I plummeted from the skies, they all danced around me, taunting me with all I had lost.

No.

I **Refuse** to let them have what I **Deserve.**

I shall not be the only one to fall; the only one to suffer this **Damnation.**
   No.
   This was **Their Fault.**
   I will take what I **Deserve.**
   I will cut myself free from the inky tar that grasps desperately at me, pleading for me to stay and keep it company, and I shall fly once more. I shall take their place amongst the stars and cast down all those who are **Undeserving.**

THE RIDDLE OF THE OLDEST ADVERSARY
Judi Moore

I was the jester to powerful kings,
I was the black cat when witches had wings.
I was the locket on my lady's breast,
I was the cursed gold in the chest.

I was the willow at the lovers' tryst,
I was the pardon the murderer missed.
I am the serpent, the eye at the crack,
If you look behind quickly I'm at your back.

All the cheaters at cards, the drunkards in bars,
All the eyes in the night know me well.
All the king's mettled horses and all his fine men
Saw my face at the moment they fell.

The answer: envy

THE GREEN-EYED MONSTER
Fi Woods

'"Jealousy," "envy"—they're such nasty words, aren't they? They somehow even *feel* horrible when you say them, as if you've got a mouthful of dirt. When people are described as being jealous or envious it always implies that they are unpleasant people best kept away from. It's even a Deadly Sin: jealousy, aka the Green-Eyed-Monster. I don't feel like a monster though, nor do I feel like a sinner. I don't see some horrific beast with fearfully glowing green eyes staring back at me from the mirror.'

It was Christmas, and Lucas McFetridge was drowning in a black hole of depression. It wasn't anything new, it had been occurring at certain times of the year for a very long time.

'Christmas, Mother's Day, birthdays—they're meant to be special days, full of happiness. I can't remember ever having that.' Lucas talked to herself, to the empty house. 'I know it's not about getting presents, it's about someone caring enough about you to take the time and make the effort to find something they know you'll like. The only things I ever unwrap are Amazon or eBay deliveries.'

Lucas always told herself that she was buying herself presents for her birthday and at Christmas, but there was no pleasure in it. As a professional photographer she'd bought herself a new top of the range camera costing over £3000. That was three years ago, and it was still in its box. She'd never even taken it out to look at it. She'd completely lost her drive and motivation, becoming wrapped in lethargy with everything involving such an effort.

The prettiness of all the street decorations, the couples walking hand-in-hand, the parents searching for things to delight their children ... Lucas couldn't cope with it. She'd barely manage a few steps before the tears started. 'They all have someone to be with. They are all cheerful and laughing. All of my "family" are getting into this too, ready for that extended family party on xmas day. All of them except me. I'm not one of them. I'm not wanted. I'll be here on my own, same as any other day, so what's the point in trying to pretend that it's a special day? Same shit, different day.'

Lucas dreaded xmas every year; it just served to remind her that she was completely alone, that she had no one who cared about her. She could picture the big family party: the smiles, laughter, and joy as presents were given and accepted. The hectic logistics of needing four sittings for xmas dinner to accommodate the number of relatives. She hadn't been a part of that for years, but the hurt still cut deep and sharp. Her flat was bereft of decorations and dinner was just an ordinary meal. She couldn't see the point in expending time, energy, and money on these things when it was only her eyes that would see and only her stomach that would get full. In fact, she might have felt cheered, and even a little festive, if she'd put in a little effort. She might even have felt a sense of satisfaction, some pride, fulfilment—all things that just might have allowed her to feel the tiniest bit good about herself. But those possibilities never even occurred to her.

Birthdays were the same: there'd been no celebrations for her 16th birthday or her 18th. Or her 21st come to that. The claddagh ring that, for generations, had been given by parents to daughters on reaching 18 years of age was something she'd bought for herself. She rarely wore it as it seemed meaningless. 'My 16th was made memorable for being thrown out of home onto the streets, on my 18th I got positive results from a pregnancy test, and on my 21st I was in the middle of a protracted court battle against social services because they'd taken my son away. Way to go.'

Birthdays and xmases were no different from each other; they were marked only by her browsing online and buying things for herself. More things that carried no joy and remained, untouched, in their boxes. They only ever emphasised the fact that there was nobody to buy her presents.

'And relationships too: I've only ever had one good relationship and that was with Tim, my son's dad. We're still really good friends and that friendship is really special to me, but he lives so far away now that I can't see him anywhere near as much as I'd like to. Talking on the phone, or even Skype so we can see each other, it's not the same as spending time with him in person. All my other relationships were bad, and each was worse than the one before. I've been single a long time now because I can no longer cope with physical contact. I don't really mind being single, it took me way too long to learn that "any relationship is better than none" wasn't true. I am very much aware though that I am a *spinster, on the shelf, past my use-by date.* I look at all the couples and wonder how on earth they managed to find each other out of so many people in the world. And I wonder why I didn't find that *someone.* Wasn't there someone for me? Y' know those couples that have been together 50 or 60 years? I am *so* jealous that they found that kind of love, that they have that kind of love. I so badly wish I'd found that. The only thing I ever really wanted was to be married: to have a husband to love and tend to, a man who would love and care for me, someone to share my life with. A huge gert meringue of a frock, and a man standing at the end of the aisle who would turn and look at me with love and adoration. "You may kiss the bride." How I'd longed to hear those words. Then the first dance and being carried over the threshold. I'd so wanted all of that. I'd always believed in the traditional values of marriage, but it was a case of "always the bridesmaid, never the bride." And now, of course, I'm too old to even be the *bridesmaid*; I'd have to be the *Old Maid of Honour*. Emphasis on the first two words there.

My "mother" always told me that nobody would ever want me, and it turns out she was right. My son yelled at me once, "You're going to end up old and lonely with nowt but a load of lost friendships." He was right too.

I've lost so many friends, good friends, over the years that I don't even know how many. Every single thing that *could* be perceived as a slight/snub/insult, even when that was absolutely not the intention, *was* taken as a negative personal comment. The fact that this was largely due to the 16 years of the emotional abuse I'd taken from my "mother" does not alter the fact. I was unable to change/diminish/dismiss what she had told me I was, and so every time this happened I turned and walked away. I'd not been able to escape her, but as an adult I could make sure that nobody had the opportunity to hurt me more than once. I burned bridges left, right, and centre, making sure there wasn't as much as a splinter left. And I had the best mates possible, the ones who told me I was part of *their* family. They invited me round for xmas and tried to celebrate my birthdays, but although I knew they were sincere I could never get past the fact that I *wasn't* part of their families. Not *really*. I wish I'd been able to accept all they offered, but I couldn't.

I look through my address book for someone to have a chat, and maybe a cuppa with, but all the names, numbers, and addresses have been completely obliterated with layer upon layer of Tippex. I try holding random pages up to the light, in hope that I'd be able see my writing from behind the mass whiteout. It didn't work. I try to scrape it off but I'd have had more chance of escaping an Alcatraz cell using only a cocktail stick. The message is clear: I made my bed and I have to lie in it.

I wish I could go back and apologise to all those people that I'd wronged so badly. It wouldn't matter if they did not accept my apology; the point is one of giving it because they deserved it. Removing people from my life gave me no way at all of contacting them, though. I think I regret all of this more than my childhood or lack of marriage. I often think about all those friends and what I threw away.

I have become what "mother" and my son told me I'd be because of *my* inability to be someone different. Events may have set me on this path, but *I* stayed on it. Changing was too difficult and behaving as if everyone viewed me the same as "mother" was too easy. A self-fulfilling prophecy if ever there was one.

I just couldn't stop comparing myself to other people, and I always came up short.'

Lucas thought for a long moment, then fetched a notepad and a pen. She sat with the pen in her hand, thinking for another long moment. 'So much to say, but I don't want to be writing a bleedin' novel. It's time to apply K.I.S.S. I reckon. Keep It Simple, Stupid. After all Stupid might as well be my middle name.'

She wrote just enough to fill one side of an A4 page, then capped the pen and tore the page out of the book. The book and pen were left on the sofa; the single page was taken upstairs with her. 'I'm worn out; I need to rest.'

A few days later the postman rang Lucas' doorbell to deliver a package. When there was no answer he wrote out the "Something for you" card and pushed the letterbox open. By reflex he immediately took a step back, 'Bloody hell. What on earth is that smell? Surely she can't be in there with *that*.' He rang the bell a couple more times and then pulled out his phone. He was told to stay where he was and that someone would be there as soon as possible.

The postie sat down on the grass verge and lit a cigarette. The police actually turned up quite quickly; the postie only had three butts poked into the grass next to him. After explaining what had happened, and giving his name and address, he was allowed to leave.

While the first officer had been talking to the postie, the other had pushed open the letterbox and knew straight away what the smell was. He called for an ambulance to attend, then together the officers made a forced entry. One stayed by the door while the other quite literally followed his nose. In Lucas' bedroom, hanging from one of the exposed beams, was her body. Pinned to her t-shirt was a sheet of A4 paper covered in scrawly writing, which was quickly scan-read to ascertain that it was a suicide note. Both officers had had the misfortune to see a few such notes over the years and had therefore become somewhat inured to suicides, but the final two sentences stayed with both men for quite some time. They were written in green biro as opposed to the blue pen of the rest of the note:

"I had so many dreams in my life and here I am: sad, lonely, and unhappy.

I, Lucas McFettridge, am the *I Wish Monster*."

MEI LIN
Diane Narraway

I worked with my father for as long as I can remember. We traded the finest silks to wealthy members of the various imperial courts. My father claimed he was related to Empress Leisa herself. Of course, it was just spiel but the rich and regal lapped it up.

I would watch the ladies of the royal courts, along the silk road, in their exquisite gowns as they queued to buy the latest finery. How I longed to dress like them. You would think that with all the money we made I would be the best-dressed trader in all of China. But no ... for the most part I had to just keep quiet and do my work, and in exchange my father fed and clothed me. Not in finery, but in the plainer garb worn by the trade boys. This would have been fine: except I was a girl. More importantly, I was a teenage girl who longed for a beautiful silk gown.

My many protests of 'But Father ...' fell, at best, on deaf ears, but were mostly greeted by his usual refrain:

'The desire you have for a gown is far less important than the coins we make trading. With all your wants I shall need as much as I can get for your dowry.'

There was no question of me taking over the family business—that honour would go to my husband. None of this stopped me wanting to dress in the finest silk.

Once a week, all the traders met up and told stories: the desert djinn who granted wishes, or rags to riches tales of plain girls who married Emperors or wealthy landowners. Once a week I got to dream. Of course, Father would always be the first to remind me that they were just stories, and the djinn were just as capable of cursing.

As I grew older and more womanly, I longed even more to dress in finery, and I tried new arguments.

'But surely, Father, it would be good advertising: I could tidy myself up and show off the merchandise.'

'Absolutely not. That would be silk I couldn't sell, and we need the money ...'

'... for my dowry. Yes, yes, yes. So you've said, a thousand times before. I don't see how I'll even find a suitor, dressed like a street boy.'

'That's enough! I won't hear any more about dresses.'

I honestly believed my father hated me. I looked like my mother, who had died bringing me into the world. I was also convinced that she would have dressed me in silk.

We always travelled the silk road in caravans, but, one day, a member of our group received word that robbers had been spotted on the favoured route, so a detour was suggested. My father seemed uneasy.

'Stay by me Bái; do not stray, and do not daydream or dawdle.'

I heard the words but took precious little notice. I was hoping that by cutting through the desert we might encounter a djinn who granted wishes.

'Bái ... Bái.'

'Yes Father. I heard you the first time.'

'You are as much of a dreamer as your mother. It was the ruin of her.'

It was the first time he had mentioned her in years.

'Stop ... Father. What do you mean? ... Father?'

"Just stay close, Bái."

I had never seen my father like this before. I was used to him constantly preaching at me about the virtues of living humbly, or the dangers of jealousy: "coveting what another has only leads to ruin."

I had no idea what he meant most of the time, but it didn't stop me obsessing over beautiful silk gowns and fine jewels. I hated dressing and eating like paupers. We were wealthy merchants, yet we lived like beggars. The other traders and merchants didn't, so why should we?

It was getting dark, and negotiating the desert was hard enough during the day, so we set up camp for the night. There were twelve of us in total, so we built a fire and shared the food around. Of course, the others lived like proper traders, so I was glad to share their food.

Women weren't allowed to trade, hence my boyish attire and name. My real name was Mei Lin, but I hadn't been called that in years. I had no idea how I was expected to get a husband, but still, my father knew best, apparently.

After we had eaten, I needed to relieve myself so, despite my father's protests, I headed to some nearby caves. In mid-flow I caught sight of a djinn out of the corner of my eye.

'It's alright child; I won't hurt you. Bring me some food later, and I will reward you handsomely.' I nodded, unable to speak—struck dumb by fear.

I did as the djinn asked, and waited till they were all asleep before sneaking out with some food for him. Truth to tell, I wasn't sure what the djinn ate, so I grabbed a bit of everything.

'Were you seen, child?'

'No, I don't think so. I waited till everyone was asleep.'

'Good, good, and thank you for the food.'

I put the food down, but I noticed the djinn didn't touch it.

'Are you not hungry?' I enquired, pointing to the food.

'Yes, yes, of course, but first I would like to repay you. Tell me child, what is your heart's desire?'

'Oh, that's easy. Above all, I would love a gown made of the finest silk.'

The following morning, my father found me lying on the cave floor, wearing the finest silk shroud, a plate of food next to my corpse.

'Oh, my beautiful Mei Lin; you are just like your mother. If only you could have trusted me, instead of envying others.'

GLUTTONY

GLUTTONY
Diane Narraway

Carbohydrate junkie!
Calorie slave!
Sticky sweet foods
Are all that you crave.
Growing out of your clothes
At an alarming rate,
And the scales clearly say
That you're overweight.
Yet still you continue
To eat more and more,
Until one day,
You fall to the floor.
Writhing in agony,
And gasping for breath,
Your excessive gluttony,
Has just caused your death!

THE CONFESSION OF SAMUEL KEEPS
Kate Knight

    This is my account of what occurred on that fateful night. Whether you believe what I say to be true or not is your choice. As you well know, I have an insatiable thirst for the pleasures of mankind; my understanding is that it's a trait inherited from my father, who committed suicide when I was an infant. He himself could not live with the horrors of what his actions did to the woman he loved. The suffering he caused did not show its ugly face until he awoke from his drunken stupor. He did not realise the enormity of the consequences until his bare foot slid on the blood from my mother's throat. I was told by many people that he was a good father and husband when he was not indulging in his many vices, but the sight of her body tipped him over the edge. He took his own life, using his leather belt as a noose. Thankfully, my mother's main artery was missed by a hair's width. The thought of leaving her child parentless willed her to survive.

    I have always been the sort of person who relishes in joy. The joy of sex and lots of it with multiple partners, the opiates that are readily available if you wander down certain dark streets in London, and the drinking of rum, which is in abundance in most areas. Residing in a room above an inn used regularly by passing sailors did not help my insatiable thirst. Not only for the warming pleasures of that brown liquid, but also the thrill of good company, interesting conversation, and a buxom whore bouncing on my knee for the price of a silver coin. I have never been short of coins: I inherited a generous amount of money from a wealthy relative when my mother finally passed being that she was the only heir. This plentiful income allowed me to live without the need for employment. I once had enough to live my whole life comfortably, but the price of pleasure soon outweighed my income. In fact, my pockets being bottomless began this spiral, which brought me to the situation I find myself in now.

It was on the tenth of May when the illustrious Lady Charlotte docked in the port not far from me. The weather was fair, and the sailors poured into the inn, seeking ale and a firm ground to steady their feet. They brought with them tales of their adventures at sea: sirens beneath the stormy waves and distant sightings of sea-monsters piercing through the mist. I have often dreamt of living such a life, but sadly I do not possess the cast-iron stomach of such men. At a guess, I would say a crowd of twenty or more sailors burst through the doors, their loud, rowdy voices echoing through the building. I had no need for sleep, so I filled my pockets with silver and headed down to join in with the merriments. As always, I was welcomed with open arms because, after months at sea, a fresh face always warranted a smile. Of course, only moments later word spread to the local whorehouse of their presence. The doors flung open yet again and in poured twelve women of all shapes and sizes, breasts bursting from their bodices, flaunting their bodies, and looking for someone to part with their silver. My face is well-known by the ladies, so naturally I had the joy of the company of my usual girl. I liked her because she held no boundaries: anything was for sale, given the right price. For me, money was no issue, and she knew it.

The drinks flowed well that evening, so much so that John the landlord sent a messenger to his son requesting help. At around eight in the evening, the sailors were singing old shanties with a drink in one hand and a girl in the other. The atmosphere was alive. I was on my seventh glass, possibly eighth, when I felt the need for carnal pleasure, so I placed my empty glass upon the bar, took my whore's hand and led her up to my room, where we indulged in sex. Soon after, she left me face up on my bed with silver in her pocket, satisfied with the night's takings. I slept for a while, but not for very long as the noise from below was deafening and even the drunken state I was in did not enable deep sleep to take hold. Sex had sobered me up somewhat, so I decided to re-join my sailor friends who were enjoying a lock-in session. For me, this was an open invitation, given my place of residence. As I entered the bar area, several sailors were already relieving their lust with their chosen woman in the seating areas, so I sat at the bar and ordered another drink. John did state that I had reached my limit for the night, but I threw down some cash and he replaced it with my usual double shot of rum. He suggested that I drink up and go back upstairs, but I did not intend to leave until the inn was empty. I always liked to be the last man standing. I expect my body was so used to alcohol that it had grown accustomed to the effects: I had not blacked out in many years.

One of the sailors took the last empty space and sat beside me at the bar. He introduced himself as Eric; he had just finished with his whore and decided to have a few more drinks. I cannot picture his face because my vision was blurred at this point, but I do remember commenting on his peculiar eyes. The whites had the usual yellow scorbutic tinge, but the irises were a deep brown, so deep that they appeared black. As the conversation flowed I expressed my love for the stories that his sort told, so in response he began to tell me a tale from his past adventures.

I will have trouble with the details, but I clearly recall him mentioning a woman in the far east who provided the sailors with a herb that relieved their carnal desires while at sea. They were usually a male-dominated crew and months without such pleasures took their toll. This naturally intrigued me, as all the female companies in the world could not satisfy my lust, especially on the rare occasion that I found myself sober. I explained that the only way to dull my urges was opiates and rum. The sailor passed me a hessian bag from his pocket and gave a price of six silver coins. I reached into my pocket and pulled out only five, so I explained that the rest was upstairs. I told him I would see to it that he got what was owed, but I had to try out my new purchase first. The sailor took the five coins and agreed.

    The bag was tied with a leather twine. I opened it up and reached inside, where my fingertips touched what felt like ground pepper. I asked my new friend how to take the substance; I was unsure whether to devour it or place it in a pipe and smoke the herb. He informed me that the most successful way to gain the desired benefits was to wet my finger, dip it into the bag and place what was on my finger under my tongue. I did so without delay.

    Instantly the effects made themself known. A tingling chill raced down my spine, stopping only at my coccyx. My belly began to churn, and I felt something stir in my private parts. Before I had time to comment on the symptoms, I felt an explosion of pleasure unlike anything I had ever experienced before. I couldn't help but call out, holding my hand tightly over my mouth to save my own embarrassment. Eric grinned knowingly. When the symptoms dissipated, I asked my friend to remain where he sat while I fetched his extra coin. He agreed without dispute and alerted the barman that he required two more glasses of rum. I left the inn and began the climb up the stairs which seemed to extend to twice the distance and steepness of before. I put it down to my drunken mind and climbed anyway. As I reached the halfway point, I looked above me to see at least one hundred more steps stretching off into the distance. I collapsed, exhausted, on the step and leant against the wall. My breathing became rapid, my heart galloped like a fleeing horse. Pain struck my chest as my heart felt like it was preparing to explode. I feared for my life. My sight faded into darkness as I gasped what felt like my last breath.

  I am not sure how much time had gone by, but when I opened my eyes the inn was silent. I assumed the merriments had come to an end. I must have been leant on those stairs the whole night. It appeared that I had fallen asleep on the third step from the top; I could clearly see my own door right above me. I pulled myself to my feet and opened the door. The shock and horror hit me all at once and I vomited over the floor of my room. Laid out upon my bed was the corpse of my whore. Her throat had been cut, I can only assume by the broken bottle that lay on the bed beside her. Her blood covered my linen and still dripped onto the wooden floorboards. Her mouth was agape displaying an expression of fear. I gathered myself together and approached the body. Something about her eyes was not quite right and as I gazed upon her pale face, I saw that two silver coins lay on each eye, holding the lids tightly shut.

    I was confused; I distinctly remember her leaving that night, I still remember the jingling of my coin in her pocket as she spun around and blew me a kiss, pulling the door to. All at once I remembered my own father. The memories of the story my mother told came rushing back. This was exactly what he did to my mother before taking his own life, only I had achieved my goal where he failed to release my mother's soul. Like me, he could not remember his actions. He explained what had happened in a note, left to my future carers. I was a mere infant sleeping in the cot beside the bed when his crime occurred, yet I was untouched. In fact, he made sure that I would not be left too long after his passing, summoning help just before he took his own life.

    It must have been me—I did it, even if I don't recall it. A son of a man who attempted murder on his own wife, I have carried on the tradition without even realising. I needed a drink to dull the shock so I left her there; she showed no signs that her life could be saved. She was gone, dead and beyond help even if I tried. The blood had all but left her, there was no taking it back.

I ran down the stairs leaving trails of her blood down the wall from my fingertips and entered the room previously occupied by the sailors, whores, John the bartender, and his son. There was no life to be seen. No life, only bodies.

As I write this confession, I am sitting on the only table that remains in this inn which is not covered with the blood of thirty victims. I know not what occurred; I only know that I am the only one whose blood still pumps freely, the only one who still breathes the air. Every face that I see around me is still, all familiar to me from the night before. Only one is missing from this macabre scene: my friend Eric, the man with the crimson eyes, but an empty hessian bag lies on the bar.

On my right, is a door to the balcony, where a hangman's noose overlooks the river, a reminder of times that have passed. It is that which will take me from this world, as the guilt is already torturing my mind. I wish to receive my punishment in hell rather than at the hands of England's lawyers. Some see my actions as a coward's way out, but to me the only punishment I am deserving of is from Satan's fire. Please, do as you will with my body, I have no need for it now. I lived my life wallowing in the sins of gluttony, but it was not just me who paid the price, scores of other people paid too. They were all sons, daughters, fathers, mothers, friends. I could wish that it had never happened, but how can I wish away something that I cannot remember.

Samuel Keeps.

CHRISTMAS, 1989
Judi Moore

And so this is Christmas.

We've dried the tears of avaricious children
who did not receive expected gifts
of consumer durables.

Just in time for the festivities
we've stuck another Band Aid
on one of the world's sore places
and, feeling this effort is enough,
plunged merrily into the trough.

We've really made the effort
because it's Christmas, after all.
We'll gobble turkey
while half the world goes hungry.
It's expected of us.

"The poor you have always with you"
is our mantra. Don't they know
you can have too much of a good thing?
Loving and giving quickly pall,
long before the twelfth day of Christmas.

*

Broadcasters have rounded up
the first, the last, the mawkish,
the best and worst, the skate-boarding duck—
tasteless fare, served up day after day,
lukewarm with the turkey.

And yet beneath the tawdry tinsel
and our determination to see no evil,
to have a good time, no matter what the cost
there is still hope. I believe I saw, just yesterday,
Romania crawl out, bloody, from the womb;

and see, the Gate at Brandenburg stands open now,
and grinning Berlin citizens with hammers
chip at the brittle blockwork of the Wall.

God rest ye merry, all.

GREED

GREED
Diane Narraway

My money, my lovely money
Surrounds me like no other.
My money, my lovely money
Means more to me than any lover.

For my money, I would beg, borrow,
Swindle, cheat, and steal.
I'd do anything for my money,
I'll agree to any shady deal.

And there are many fancy gems,
And priceless works of art,
But it's money that I really love,
And preferably unmarked.

So, pile the dollars higher and higher,
Let me revel in my cash,
And please, Lady Fortuna,
Just don't let Wall Street crash.

AN OWN GOAL
G. W. Hawker

PART 1

Through my binoculars, I caught the exact moment the snare took. At first, the buck appeared to pause, surprised at his sudden restriction. Then the struggle started. He pulled this way and that in frantic desperation, until I could clearly see a ribbon of blood blooming on the caught hoof. I waited an hour before I strolled up to him. By now, he was exhausted and, although he made a final attempt at escape, I could see his energy was spent. This roebuck was a magnificent creature, diminutive as deer go but its tawny coat was soft and comforting to touch. He was looking at me with his big black eyes as I plunged the knife into his throat. At first he shuddered in disbelief. By the fifth stab, I could see his body was surrendering to the inevitable and his head with its crown of antlers slumped into my lap. Covered in his blood, I walked back to the house, satisfied that, at the very least, this beast would never chomp my lawn again.

More than anything else, Willow House symbolised the extent of my success. It was built from scratch, with the money I earned from fifteen years of Premiership football. Some of my old team-mates squandered their cash on having a good time (often falling for their own snares of alcohol, drugs or gambling), while others wasted their bounty on poor relationship choices. Not me though; I didn't make those same mistakes: when Lucy got too close, her beady eyes obviously set on my fortune, I sent her a vicious text which made it clear that I never wanted to see her again. 'But,' Liam said, 'I don't get it; you said you loved her.' Liam was the only friend left who I trusted. 'I did, I do, but not to the point where she could get her hands on all this.' He shrugged, but I knew what I was doing.

Starting each morning by touring Willow House was a daily luxury I was proud of. Walking along the corridor which ran from one end to the other still held the pleasure of novelty, and the delight of luxury. There are four bedrooms in each of two wings, both wings leading off the lounge, which is in the centre of the structure. This room, with its floor to ceiling windows opening onto a veranda, was the House's crowning glory, looking over my grounds like a huge eye. The morning ritual was as close to being religious as I would ever get.

After the circuit, I would go straight to the gym for no less than an hour. From there, I went to the pool, not pausing until at least a kilometre had been achieved. Except for the chef and the physio, everyone else: the gardeners, the cleaners, etc was paid the minimum wage. Why waste money? But the chef kept him happy. You never mess with someone who's responsible for the food on your plate. I don't see him from one week to another, but as long as the meals magically appear, I frankly don't care. The same logic applies to the physio: to maintain my level of fitness, I need to know I can trust someone to manipulate my muscles and maximize their vigour. Life is long. Life is short. Whichever is true, while I am here I will conserve the gifts that have come my way.

*

As you may have guessed, I'm not one for change. Two changes in a week were unwelcome. When I didn't answer my mother's call, she left a message saying that both of my parents were going to pay a visit that weekend. Mother finished the message with the banality that "you only have one set of parents." Thank Christ for that. Ever since my career had taken off, they had been like flies around the honey-pot. They used to be more than happy in their council house, but as soon as the capital began to flow, every encounter hid some hint about wanting this or needing that. It was rather pathetic. Other than the usual occasions - Christmas, birthdays, anniversaries - I decided early on not to spend one penny on them. Despite my mother's pleas for more contact, I knew that they wanted something more from me.

The second disruption was that my physio Alton resigned. He was pregnant - or rather his wife was - and he needed to widen his clientele in order to make ends meet. I was about to refuse him the much-needed reference when he volunteered a replacement. Ella Callaway was just out of her training, but already had a robust reputation. 'I know she's currently looking for work and she's available for your Thursday session should you want to try her out?' Although it sounded like Alton couldn't wait to get away from me, I agreed to give her a chance on a provisional basis only, of course. 'As she is newly qualified,' I added, 'I'll put her on a temporary wage.' I mentioned a figure that was about half of what I was paying him. Take it or leave it.

Thursday came and Ella Callaway arrived ten minutes late. "Time is money", as they say. I was none too happy and would have sacked her before she started if it hadn't been for a tender calf muscle I wanted relief from.

Ella began her therapy far too tentatively. If it wasn't causing a little pain, I couldn't see that it would be any use. I was about to push her away when suddenly, as if hearing my thoughts, she started digging into my muscles with focussed precision. For one so slight, the jab from her elbow was excruciating. Once, she actually sat astride me and poured her weight into the shoulders, squeezing the breath out of me. Exhilarating.

I generally didn't enjoy conversation when having treatment. Ella must have been of like-mind because, other than introductions and directional input, she hardly opened her mouth.

'Where you from?' I asked her at the end of the session, towelling myself down.

'I don't think you would know it. Ludlow?'

'Shropshire. With a castle.'

'That's right. Shropshire with a castle.'

It was the first time she smiled. And it was the first time I could see that, under her rather dour persona, there was beauty of sorts, a quiet, natural beauty. I booked her for the following Monday.

PART 2

It took over a year but, despite my reservations and concerns, I proposed to Ella Callaway, and she accepted. In all that time, Ella had not expressed one comment about my wealth. She was the most unmaterialistic woman I had ever met. She seemed to be content to live in her one-bedroom flat on the other side of town, turning up in her Fiat 500 twice a week to manipulate my muscles with a skill that was almost mystical. Her techniques were original and testing. She literally put her whole self into the session. Twice she fell onto the floor and gave herself a nosebleed. Occasionally she came in with bruising on her face, which I put down to her exuberance from some other session. She always laughed it off as "nothing."

Gradually, over the year, the intimacy of contact worked in both our favours, and I became her exclusive client. Her touch sent me wild; the final massage, intimate and sweaty, would leave me relaxed and fulfilled and ready for any demands or challenges the day may hold for me. Of course, I took precautions.

Three days before the wedding, I called her into the office. My solicitor, Bob Campion, was in attendance as I showed her the pre-nuptial agreement. It clearly stated that, in the unlikely event of a divorce, I would retain Willow House and all assets accrued prior to our marriage. In the likely event of children, I would hold full custody but would never deny access. She would return to her flat and all would be well. Although initially shocked by this ambush, Ella was as good as gold and signed the contract without protest or comment. We uncorked a bottle of inexpensive champagne to seal the deal.

The wedding was intentionally low-key. I wasn't one of those stupid people who would waste a hundred grand on a single ceremony. The registrar came to the house and we were married in the garden. We invited seven other people, including both sets of parents, which was more than enough. The wedding was the first time my parents had met Ella. We had Skyped once or twice, which negated travelling across the country; an unnecessary journey which wouldn't have made any difference to anything. Her parents, seeing Willow House in all its splendour, were overawed by the obvious opulence of the place. When they did speak, out would come another compliment of some sort. I wallowed in it all. Sycophants do have their uses.

Looking very sure of himself, Liam arrived in a three-piece suit which must have cost him as much as the whole wedding. He always liked wasting cash. Then there were two of Ella's friends, Susie, and Delta. Delta was tall, with long black hair touching her waist. I feigned interest in her business plan to play the exchange markets, and invited her to contact me. You never know, I may be able to advise.

The day went as predicted: we all had too much to drink, but this helped my speech to go down well. Looking at the guests, in our vast dining room, I was genuinely gratified, to the point where the feeling "happiness" flashed through my mind and coursed through my body. Life was good. Life was very good indeed.

*

I began getting the nightmares about a couple of months later, clueless as to its possible cause. Ella and I had eased into a routine which suited us. Most weekdays she went off, visiting friends for coffee, while I kept myself fit or serviced my investments. Occasionally, I met up with Liam for a drink, or shot a round of golf with a few colleagues. The latter were carefully selected to ensure that no one had a handicap better than mine. I was even up for the odd game of football, though that was a rarity. I tended to avoid football these days, as it was an open invitation to injury. Living a fairly uncluttered life in which I had the control, there was no ready answer as to why my sleep was disturbed by nightmares. Ostensibly everything was in order: the transition to marriage had gone seamlessly, business was brisk, and my body fat was down to a healthy 14%.

The nightmares always started the same, though the ending varied. I am walking in my grounds when my foot becomes caught in a snare. As I pull against its grip the snare became tighter with every tug. If I try to use my fingers to loosen the trap, they become caught too. Often the dream ends with me covered in blood. I look back at the empty house, hoping that someone will see me. I shout for Ella, but she never appears. In the most traumatic endings, endings in which I wake up sweating, my struggle becomes so intense that my foot is completely severed and I fall screaming to the ground.

'Maybe you should see a doctor, perhaps a psychiatrist?' insisted Liam, more than once. 'What does Ella say?' 'Nothing,' I told him, 'I haven't told her.' Liam raised his eyebrows in his comic way, 'Perhaps it's just a phase. Or the reason for them will come to you when you're ready.'

Liam knew what he was saying. A week passed, and, as if to compensate, I had started running longer distances, up to ten kilometres at a time. My favourite run took me into the nearby woods. Today I smashed the 45-minute mark, but as I was walking up the drive, cooling off, I was surprised to see Liam's car parked next to a BMW. Approaching the front door, I was greeted by a man I didn't recognise. He introduced himself with a smug smile on his face: 'Gerald Smart from Taylor and Smart Solicitors. I'm solicitor for the Plaintiff.'

'What the hell are you talking about?' I asked him.

'I'm serving papers on you, my friend.'

'What papers?'

'Divorce.'

That took the smile from my face. 'What the fuck are you talking about?'

Smart was explaining, but the words sounded like different language in which I only understood the odd phrase. Ella was seeking a divorce on the grounds of incompatibility and cruelty. Smart handed me photographs of Ella's injuries, which included shots of her nosebleeds and bruising.

'Your wife,' continued Smart, 'will have possession of Willow House until a satisfactory resolution has been reached.'

'No fucking way!'

Liam and Ella suddenly appeared on the veranda above us, his arm around her shoulder. Smart explained there was indeed a fucking way: Ella was pregnant, and it was due before Christmas. A judge had made an interim order. The locks had already been changed, and all of his assets were frozen. In a spirit of generosity, Ella was "more than happy" for him to use her one-bedroom flat for the time being. Furthermore, she had thrown in her old Fiat 500, mothballed in one of his garages. Smart dangled a ring of keys in front of him.

'But,' I shouted, trying to muster a laugh, 'But I have a pre-nup in place: she gets nothing.'

'I wondered when you would mention the pre-marital agreement,' Smart said, dropping the keys at my feet. 'It was signed under duress, only three days before the ceremony. Consent therefore was not valid. Not worth the paper it was written on, I'm afraid.'

I pulled back from Smart and looked up to the two of them. 'Why have you done this, Ella?' I yelled, an irritating plea in my voice. 'You had everything.' Ella smiled as Liam leant forward on the wall, 'Your greed made you blind.'

'My greed?' I screamed at him. 'How about your bloody greed?'

This time Ella spoke.

'Oh, my greed helped me see the possibilities. Don't worry, you'll have your day in court.' She turned and walked back into the house.

The snare bit so hard into my flesh, I fell onto the ground. This could simply not be happening, but as the door was slammed in my face, I realised in that one terrible moment that life would never be the same again. Money is wasted on the rich.

LUST

LUST
Scarlett Paige

Twist me in a lucid dream,
Make me sweat,
Make me scream.
Cover me in depraved desire,
Stoke the flames,
Fan the fire.
Feel the heat of wanton lust,
Do with me
What you must.
Swear and curse
With bitter rage,
In words from
A forgotten age.
Make me writhe,
Jerk, and wrench.
I'll be your wytch,
I'll be your wench,
I'll be here till the end of time,
With passion beyond
Reason and rhyme.
And all the while you dominate,
Take control,
And subjugate.
I'll be whatever you need,
Make me burn,

And make me bleed,
And all the while
You're in control.
I will yield,
And I will fold.
And oh,
How much I'll beg and plead,
Just for you to spill your seed.
When all is done
And you are spent,
You will weep,
And to your God repent.
And as I drain you completely dry,
I can hear your Spirit cry.
Call me succubus,
Call me daemon,
Who comes to you
As darkness deepens.
So, call to me within your dreams,
And enjoy it while
It's me who screams.
For I am the beast
Within your heart,
That will, one day,
Tear your mortal soul apart.

DOLLY LANE
Diane Narraway

"Last night it was cold out on the street, an' all of us workin' girls were desperate to earn a bob or two for a night's lodgin'. Ours is a simple life: we bend over, lie dahn, 'itch our skirts up an' for a few moments we're a release, a means to their end. Our 'ole reason for existence is to literally fill an 'ole in some gentleman's life. Now there's a misnomer if ever there was, these gentlemen are rarely gentlemen, most of 'em are just drunks. Still, a quart of gin will always take the edge off it, no matter 'ow old you are; except you 'as to earn the price of it first.

Me name's Dolly, Dolly Anderson, an' I was born on these streets. Me mother was a workin' girl, but 'er mother—well now, she was a showgirl. She was on the stage an' everythin.' Famous she was, a singer an' dancer, an' accordin' to me mother she was beautiful, 'ad gentleman swoonin' after 'er she did. Proper gents, not like that lot round Dosset Street. I'm named after 'er, but I don't 'ave 'er talent, not a bit of it. Well, I can sing but I never learned to dance; there's not much need of either on these streets. Me mother said I 'ad two left feet, not entirely sure what it meant, but I doubt it was a compliment. She wasn't big on compliments, she always said 'Compliments don't pay your rent!' An' while it would 'ave been nice to 'ave been told I looked nice, or 'ad done somethin' well when I was younger, I 'ave to concede she was right. I don't need to be told I look pretty; I just need the money for a warm bed an' an 'ot meal on a cold wintry night such as last night.

Last night, one I'll never forget it, was a warm bed most of us were workin' for; a thrupenny knee-trembler would see you right, an' a couple of fuckers would get you an extra blanket an' a quart of gin. That was all we wanted on cold nights. The rooms weren't plush, pretty much all our lodgin's we shared wiv each other, an' all of 'em we shared wiv rats, mice, an' mites. Still, as long as there was gin an' some warmth, we weren't complainin', an' it was an 'ole lot better than sleepin' in doorways or on a tupenny rope.

Earlier on, I'd been workin' on Duval Street, or Dosset Street as we still called it, dahn near the passageway by Miller's Court. I 'ated that area, most of us did. Y'see there were still some who could remember the night Mary Kelly was murdered. I couldn't, I was only a babe back then an' since then the street 'as been renamed but it still feels ... well ... uncomfortable. I s'pose that's the best way to describe it. There's always an eerie chill in the air, especially at night, an' all of us are superstitious. We all carry trinkets, good luck charms for protection, such as we 'ave; that an' a sharp knife. I carry a locket in me petticoat pocket, an' a knife in me boots. I wouldn't dare wear it for fear of it bein' stolen or lost; it was me gran'mother, Dolly, what owned it first. Me mother said it were given to 'er by one of 'er gentlemen friends. She believed it were given to 'er by Charles Dickens, but as lovely as that sounded, I doubted it was true. Still, it's pretty an' makes a fine good luck charm, an' I'm still 'ere so it must work.

An' the knife?

Well, y'never know when you might need it. What if Jack came back, or you copped one like 'im? Y' know what I'm sayin'?

Anyway, I'd been stood around 'opin' for a customer for a good 'our or so wivout so much as a roller* passin' by, let alone a toff or swell. Our business, if you can call it a business, is based on lust. Like I said earlier, I fill an 'ole—literally! I soothe the desires of men who seek somethin' dark an' dirty, men whose pretty wives is a little too prim an' proper for their tastes. I am there for men who are unwanted, those who lack the confidence to court a lady of their own class. Sometimes, there'd be one who liked to ride the rump, but fortunately they weren't too common, I've never 'ad one, but like wiv most fings in the Chapel, I'd 'eard talk. Then there's those who 'ave loved an' lost—they are the best type. They will take us to 'otels, not posh ones but off the street for the night, an' more often than not get you an 'ot meal too.

As it 'appened, by about 10 o'clock last night I'd earned me bed an' gin wiv a couple of rollers, a thrupenny upright, an' a bottom wetter. The last one 'ad paid well: 5 shillin's, which considerin' we'd only been dahn an alley was good money. I think 'e may 'ave been embarrassed, an' was payin' for me silence, so to speak. Either way, 5 bob is a decent earnin'. It was late an' I was 'eaded to the local ale 'ouse when I encountered a toff. 'E was soft- spoken, one of those rare gems: a widow who 'ad no interest in findin' a wife, but every interest in payin' for 'some comfort', as 'e put it.

I already 'ad enough for an 'alf-decent room an' a good meal, an' I didn't need the money so much, but 'e was nice: gentlemanly, an' offered to buy me dinner first. It'd been a while since anyone treated me this kindly, so I agreed. 'E was true to 'is word, a slap-up dinner in a posh restaurant. As you can imagine, all eyes was on me as the *Matrey-somethin'* mumbled 'Certainly Sir' an' showed us to a table in a dimly candlelit corner. They might've let me *in*, but they didn't want me ruinin' the look of the place in me tattered old rags. I've never eaten so much, nor so well. The food was *squizit*. I fink that's the right word. Afterwards 'e took me to a fancy 'otel. It was a 10, maybe 15,-minute walk, but we chatted a lot. 'E actually seemed genuinely interested in me.

Nobody 'ad ever asked about me—me 'opes, an' fears, except the other girls of course. Me biggest fear, of course, was same as all us girls: the prospect of Jack returnin', or one like 'im.

Wherever we went, they knew 'im, but only ever addressed 'im as Sir. The 'otel let us in the back door, on account of me I s'pose. There's no mistakin' what I am; no amount of powder an' rouge can 'ide that.

What did I call 'im?
Well, 'e told me 'is name was Arfur, but I doubt it was 'is real name. People rarely tell us their real names an' so long as they pay us, we don't care; same goes for those few toffs who are regulars.

'E opened the door for me an' gestured for me to sit dahn. The room was beautiful, wiv a soft chair in the corner, which I sank into while 'e busied 'imself in the closet. The 'ole room was lavish: there was gas lamps an' runnin' water.

"Wash yourself, but slowly—I like to watch," 'e said, "And afterwards, you can put this on."

I obliged but kept me boots on; us girls always keep our boots on. You never know when you might need to run, from a Jack, the mutton shunters, or a violent customer. It's all the same an' customers knows it, even this one.

'E lay a fine silk dress on the bed, delicately decorated wiv tiny pink flowers, ribbons, an' bows. It was gorgeous an' I nodded, too stunned to speak. I 'ad never seen such luxury, let alone experienced it; the room, the dress: it was overwhelmin.' 'Owever, I did as 'e said an' 'e sat in the chair an' watched, noddin' an' mumblin' gestures of approval 'ere an' there. I paid special attention to me breasts an' cunny, an' 'e seemed to like that.

I could see 'e was aroused an' once 'e deemed me clean enough 'e nodded for me to get dressed. "Only the dress, no under-garments," 'e added before 'e lay me on the bed an' 'itched up me skirt. I wriggled in assistance. 'E was gentle, which was somethin' I was far from used to. Most men are in an' out, kecks buttoned an' off dahn the street as quick as a 'ook wiv a mutton shunter behind 'em. But not this one. This one took 'is time, kissin' me feet an' workin' 'is way up to me cunny. I squealed in delight, no one 'ad ever kissed me there before, not even one of the other girls. I'd over'eard conversations, gigglin' an' even breathless moans, but I'd never been on the receivin' end—until now. 'E responded, lickin' faster an' faster, an' me heartbeat proper loud and quick, then wivout warnin' everythin' changed. I felt 'is teeth, 'ard an' sharp, as 'e bit into me upper thigh, narrowly missin' me cunny. I jumped wiv the pain, an' 'e flipped me over. I thought for a minute 'e may be a bottom wetter, but I was so very wrong.

The room spun as 'e entered me. 'E was no longer gentle as 'e roughly rode the rump, clawin' an' bitin' into me skin. I was in agony, but from somewhere, deep inside me, I managed to reach inside me right boot. As I said, the Chapel 'as been on edge since the Ripper. It may 'ave been 17 years ago, an' I may only 'ave been a babe at the time, but I'd 'eard enough stories to know 'e'd never been caught, an' that complacency can get a girl killed. I grabbed me knife an' shivved 'im straight in the shin, 'ard as I could. I must've caught 'im a good'un, because 'e stopped an' dropped to the floor. I was terrified, but took me chance an' stabbed 'im a couple more times, in the neck, before stumblin' back at the 'orror of me actions, an' fallin' into the chair. Me 'eart was thumpin', as I watched 'im bleed out. I've never killed a man an' I don't mind tellin' ya I was shakin' life a leaf, threw up a couple a times too. Watchin' the life drain out of someone, well it ain't nat'ral is it? Tears rolled down my cheeks an' I weren't sure whether I was cryin' for 'im, I mean a life's a life, when all's said an' done, or if I was cryin' on account of me bein' terrified. I needed to think.

    I sat there mesm'rised for ages; I mean, it could 'ave been minutes or 'ours, I've no idea 'ow long it was. All I remember was me arse was sore from the poundin' 'e'd given it, an' me 'ead was spinnin' as I sat lookin' at 'is corpse lyin' on the bedroom floor. I needed to do somethin', an' quickly, before daylight came an' the 'otel became aware of the situation. I may be an 'ore, but I'm no murderer—although I doubt the beak would see it that way. This man was 'ighly respected, an' by all accounts well-to-do. I stood no chance: I'd killed a toff an' I'd be 'ung for it, pure an' simple. Me 'ands was shakin' an' I could barely move. It was as if I was rooted to the spot. I reckon I musta talked meself into movin', 'cos eventually I took a deep breath an', Lord knows 'ow, managed to wash me knife.

I took a butchers in the closet an' found a clean dress, an' silk stockin's; there was, after all, plenty to choose from. Of course, I rifled 'is pockets first. A girl's gotta eat, an' the least 'e owed me was a night off of the streets. I found 'is wallet an' purse, I didn't really expect to find much, as everyone knew toffs rarely carried much. 'Owever, I did find way more than expected, £257.00 to be exact I may not be able to read, but I can count: 50 large white fivers, 2 quid in 'is wallet, an' 3 guineas, an' 2 small brass keys in a small brahn leather purse. The keys 'ad writin' on, an' although I can't read I recognised the shape of the words or rather the numbers. I'd seen one before, on a man in the local ale 'ouse. 'E was drunk an' foolishly tellin' one of the local 'ooks what it was: a safety deposit key for the National Safety Deposit Company on Queen Victoria Road. This toff 'owever, 'ad two.

I got dressed in the finest dress I could find, keepin' me old petticoat on to 'ide the notes in, an' dug around for a more *womanly* purse an' sure enough, I found one. It was a bit of a mystery why 'e 'ad so much feminine 'coutrimen's, 'e 'adn't initially seemed like a molly, but 'is actions suggested 'e might be. After all, a molly would ride the rump, an' 'e was certainly aggressive enough to suggest 'e 'ated women. Whatever the reason, I was glad 'e 'ad fine dresses, as it was me ticket out of there.

I managed to leave the 'otel unnoticed; a fine dress, it would appear, opens many doors. I guess it's true what me mother said, *clothes really do make a man* or woman. I boldly strode out the front door an' into the street leavin' Arfur, or whatever 'is name was, upstairs brahn bread. O' course, I knew the bobbies would be lookin' for 'is murderer, but I 'oped I'd be long gone. Besides, they'd be lookin' for a street girl, an' I was, to all intent an' purpose, a toff. I, Dolly Lane, am a woman of substance. Yes, I thought I'd take me gran'mother's name an' a ship, perhaps to the Americas. First things first though, I need to investigate these safety deposit boxes. I need to know just 'ow rich I am.

I flagged dahn an 'ackney usin' me wages from earlier last night, an' before long I was a good mile away from the murder scene. Don't get me wrong, this wasn't cold-blooded murder. I ain't no killer, but then 'e weren't nothin' more than an 'alf 'our gentleman. I reached the Safety Deposit Company an' showed the keys to the gentleman behind the counter. I was careful not to say too much as I felt sure, pretty dress or no, me East End accent would arouse suspicion. I nodded an' coughed, implyin' I 'ad a chill; perhaps I was a natural actress, like me gran'mother after all, as they seemed to accept it an' wivin minutes, I was left alone in the vault. I was grateful for the gentleman tellin' me to take as long as I needed, as I knew it would take me a while to find two boxes.

I felt safe in the vault. The bobbies would 'ardly be lookin' for a grubby street girl in the 'eart of London's prestige deposit box company, an' in 'ere I wasn't anythin' other than a lady wiv a slight sniffle. Eventually I found 'em: one box was slightly larger than the other. I ran me fingers across the black, lacquered surface: it was beautiful, wiv a decorative gilt lock; everythin' about the dead man in the posh 'otel screamed money. I opened the smaller one first. As I turned the key, all I could 'ear was me 'eart thumpin' in me chest, which grew louder an' louder as I slowly lifted the lid, savourin' every moment. Inside, there was jewellery, more fivers, and somethin' I couldn't identify. I replaced it in the box, as I think it may 'ave 'ad 'is name on, but I couldn't be sure. The money an' what trinkets I could, I 'id in me petticoat, an' the rest of the gems I put in me newly acquired purse. I didn't know if they were real, but I intended to find out; besides, they were, if nothin' else, very pretty an' would look good on any lady.

The second box I opened faster, as I was excited to see what else there was, but as I gazed upon the contents me 'eart stopped. I stumbled back an' dropped to the floor. It was all I could do not to throw up there an' then; I probably wouldv'e, if I 'adn't thrown up earlier. I was shaken though, I can tell you. It's 'ard to say exactly what I felt, on account of me 'ead spinnin' an' me thoughts racin' round like Lord knows what. I seem to 'ave spent most of last night on the verge of an 'eart attack, don't I? But it's a lot to cope with in one lifetime, let alone one night.

Anyway, inside the box was blood-soaked rags, stockin's p'rhaps, an' as long as I live I'll never shake the image of an 'uman 'eart, along wiv some other body parts. If it wasn't bad enough to look at, it smelt bleedin' vile, proper rancid, like it 'ad been there for years. When I finally plucked up the courage to take another butchers, I 'itched up me skirt an' 'eld it over me face; that was when I seen it. In amongst all the other stuff was somethin' what looked like a book, although it was too bloody to be sure. I mean, it looked like a butcher's shop in there. Lord knows 'ow long I'd sat on the floor wiv me 'ead spinnin' an' wonderin' what I should do, but once I seen the book somethin' snapped inside me, an' I decided there an' then on me course of action.

I locked the first box and then dropped the key to the first box inside the second box, an' locked that up too, replaced 'em an' left. An' that's when I came 'ere. That's it, that's me confession, so to speak. So, did you go there? Did you find the boxes?"

"Well, yes Miss Lane, we did, and I've got to ask, why didn't you bring us both keys? I mean why put the second one in the first box? Why not just bring us both the keys?"

"Truthfully, I wasn't sure if I'd come 'ere or not. I may have changed me mind, an' just posted it, or 'anded it in an' left. I mean, I wanted to do the right thing an' all, but I can't say as I'm too fond of the idea of being 'ung."

"I see. Well Miss Lane, 'butcher's shop' is a fair description of it, and you were right: it was a book you saw. Furthermore, despite the amount of blood on it, we found an inscription in it ..."

"A what?"

"It was given to someone as a gift, so it had their name in. Well, actually, it had a few names in it."

"Whose names?"

"It appears that it was originally given to your grandmother, Dolly Lane, by no less than Charles Dickens himself, and she passed it on to, what I suppose is, your mother Betty Anderson. After that, there are a few other names, but only one that we can make out 'Mary' ... 'Mary Kelly'."

"Blimey, so me gran'mother knew Charles Dickens after all? An' I can 'ardly bring meself to ask ... but is the toff in the 'otel what's brahn bread ... is 'e ... well ... is 'e Jack? You know ... the Ripper?"

"Yes, we believe he is."

"What's 'is name? I mean 'is real name?"

"I can't tell you that. I mean, it's not something we've been told, but let's just say he's important—high ranking and official. If you know what I mean?"

"Not really ... so ... what 'appens now?"

"Well, we think it best, Dolly Anderson, that you take the jewels and money, and go and start your new life in the Americas as Dolly Lane, like you intended. And we never speak of this again. How does that sound?"

"What? I'm not for the drop? I'm free and ... well ... rich?"

"That's about the size of it, Dolly. Here's your stuff, now get out of here and enjoy your new life. Go!"

"I could kiss you Constable ... Constable?"

"Smithson, Miss Lane ... Constable Smithson."

"Well, Constable Smithson, there is one thing I'd like t' know. What was the book?"

"Sorry, I believe it was impossible to tell. But the next tale I want to hear is that of the actress and star of the music hall, Dolly Lane."

It was early mornin', on the 12th of January 1906, when Dolly Anderson set sail for the Americas, from Southampton on the luxurious RMS Adriatic; 12 short weeks later, Miss Dolly Lane arrived in New York.

*

Dear Constable Smithson,

    I write to you with great sadness in my heart, as I regrettably inform you of the death of my wife, known to you as Miss Dolly Lane.

    It can feel no stranger for you to receive this letter than it is for me to send it, as in order to relay to you the tale of Dolly Lane, I must include some of my own story.

    I first met Dolly when she arrived in New York. She had literally just stepped off the boat, as I was securing my passage to England for the following day. She bumped into me, and as clichéd as it sounds, our eyes met and we were drawn to each other. I helped her find her way around the city that night, and we discovered we shared much in common.

    I, like her, had been brought up by my mother and never known my father, who had abandoned us when I was young and returned to England. My mother claimed he was British aristocracy: a count, baron, or some such nobility. In any conversation regarding my father, she would always end it with, "and good riddance I say!" He was apparently violent towards her and particularly brutish in the bedroom. However, he was well to do, and I was heading to England as he had recently passed away, and I was his sole beneficiary. Had my mother not recently departed herself, I'm sure she would've been quite delighted to hear of him leaving this world. It would appear that one of the girls he had been brutish to had got the better of him. Something, which no doubt, also would've given her great pleasure. 'His comeuppance', I believe is the phrase.

Anyway, upon my return to New York I sought out Dolly, who informed me of her ambition to be a singer, like her grandmother, although she believed that her grandmother was far more talented. I must confess, I was baffled. Dolly had money, and plenty of it, so did not need to eke out a living in music halls. Still, who was I to judge?

I had a friend who ran one of the more prestigious concert halls, but after a short stint there it became too tame for Dolly; she wanted more. More of what, I wasn't sure, but she was. Burlesque, that's what she wanted to be doing, and she secured a position in a 'speakeasy' downtown. I attended every performance. Where Dolly went, I followed, like a lovesick puppy. I watched her be wined and dined by New York's elite, hanging off the arms of celebrity gangsters, and bootleggers. Dolly was in her element.

By the end of Prohibition, Dolly was legendary. She had carved her name across the heart of New York City, but even she knew she was too old for burlesque. So, she returned to the music halls as a singer. Sadly, like most 'speakeasy' singers and dancers, she was yesterday's news; too old to strip and too forgotten to be worthy of proper employment. She had ridden the high life of champagne and cocaine and was now hurtling towards Skid Row.

I couldn't let my beautiful Dolly spend her days trying to secure work in a city that had forgotten her, so I asked her to marry me, and her agreement made me the happiest man ever. We were wed on the 1st of March 1925; Dolly was 39, and I was 45 years of age. We spent 20 years together, prior to her death, but I'd loved her since that cold, January day, in 1906, at Brooklyn Dockyard. She was, and always will be, my sweet Dolly Lane.

It were on her deathbed that she mentioned her promise to you, and asked that I write a letter to you, telling her story. It was the drink you see: it took hold of her, and ate away at her until there was nothing left of the woman I knew. I must confess that I have never really known what brought her to New York, although I am very grateful that it did. And as for my deceased father ... well, as my mother would say, 'good riddance.' So, here is her story; at least, from my point of view, and such as I can tell you.

MY SWEET DOLLY LANE
Diane Narraway

Dolly, Oh Dolly
My sweet Dolly Lane
Enriched my life at
The height of her fame

Her beauty shone out
Like a lamp in the dark
And the songs she sang
Captivated my heart

With elegance and grace
She danced on the stage
A sophisticated butterfly
In a gilded iron cage

She hung off the arms
Of gangsters and stars
In seedy motels
And speakeasy bars

The price of her company
Cocktails and champagne
Caviar and honey
Opiates and cocaine

The most graceful dancer
A beautiful chanteuse
To all she entertained
she was surely their muse

But Dolly, how quick
you became yesterday's news
Cos the high life's only high
When you don't need to use

So, where neon signs once
Shone out her name
The neon lights on the streets
Instead show her shame

Oh, Dolly sweet Dolly
Such is the refrain
That tells of the life
Of my sweet Dolly Lane.

   Yours faithfully,

    William John Albert-Poole

     *

Sadly, the letter was returned, 'not known at this address', and Dolly's story was never told.

LUST TO DUST
Bekki Milner

Moonlight drapes through the window, casting long shadows of the frame across the bed, like the bars of a jail cell. A simple white sheet melts over the limbs that lie beneath, gathered like icy snow drifts in the hot curve of a hip, the sensual swerve of a shoulder, scented with stardust and sweat, damp with lust. A hand emerges, finds its way over skin, following the hills and valleys to the secret sweet space between her thighs, invoking silky sighs against the pillow.

Who knows how many nights the lovers lay upon the bed? Entangled below a lust-fuelled and lazy haze, they devour their need for each other, feeding the hunger that rests in their loins, ignoring the starvation in their bellies. They twist, tumble, and moan, the sheet sliding to their feet as they meet again, and again, and again.

Their pleasure forms in torrid waves, rolling and crashing against the headboard, drawn by the moon, just like the tide. Their skin shines with need and effort, their bodily obligations ignored for the spell of ardour each cast over the other the moment that they met.

Night becomes day, day becomes night, the sheet yellowed with sweat, hair tangled and matted. The lovers lie still, breast to breast, heart to heart; a conjoined drum-beat that once threatened to break through their ribs is now faint and slow, a dance drawing to a close.

Finally, the lovers sleep, entwined like vines around a tree, locked together at the knees. Joined in death, their final moans their vows, consummated by lust. A shadow sweeps over their cold bodies, the shine of a scythe that lay in wait for the two-backed-beast to lead the lovers to their fate.

THE QUEEN AND THE JAILOR
Defoe Smith

In his mind he constantly rants to himself, but on the outside the head jailor is cool and collected. He seems to play it by the book and is committed to being impeccable in every aspect of duty. All the time he plans, he beats himself up over what he has done. Two sides on a coin, two sides on a card, and two sides to a story ...

"Have you ever sat and truly wished you had what your heart desperately desires, even if that meant destroying all that you knew? Would you risk such a thing?

"It matters not whether there will be anything left afterwards; a glimpse, a sign, or a certain look behind the mask, which is covering any evidence, other than that stone-piercing glare from those cold blue eyes! Everything is lost to temptation!

"That isn't my particular sin, but many others fall to the wayside of temptation every day, which I used to exact my revenge! But now what? Every day I see the results of my actions, and although at first I took great pride in achieving my goal, that changed.

"Now, as the years have passed and I have made my way through rank and file, I sit down and watch her game; I see the way she is constantly tormented by the cards' handlers. It was never meant to be easy, for when is revenge sweet in any sense... for either party?"

"There's no easy way to correct what has been done My true love has long been lost by way of the cards, and time has turned me into the cold-hearted monster that sits and exacts tiny portions of revenge every single day! What choice is left? As the master guard for the house of Clubs, I execute the house's will ... to the last!"

"Every day I see the mechanics of man and know what makes him tick tick tick like a clock, yet I cannot see my own!"

"I've got one chance at this one chance to escape, or one chance to see my plans come to fruition. There's no time to hang around if I want to relish the rewards, for the rewards aren't watching the victim squirm and suffer in my wicked dealings. They aren't even what I gain in material possession. The riches lay where my severed conscience once thrived, remember that thing?"

"So, I lost my first through being forbidden her love, then I thought I would devote my life to exacting revenge. But when that was done, I realised that I had actually kippered myself up more than anyone else!"

"So how many years has it taken to realise?"

"How many valuable tears spent?"

"Day after day I see my victim trapped inside a magickal prison in the form of a deck of cards and there's no end in sight. If you think about it long enough, all of the days and nights spent wooing her and I broke my own rule: I got attached!"

"In all of known history no one has ever escaped or been released from the deck, and there is no way of escaping that I know of, even after studying the workings. Yet this is the only conclusion: I'll help her escape ... topple the house and change the world forever."

Meanwhile, to her ex-Royal Highness, the Queen of Hearts, her card is a cell! A square room so it appears, it rocks and tumbles during set times of the day but at night it is cold, dark, and still. All the contents of the cell including the occupant were strewn about and, in the centre, she sits dishevelled on the floor.

Time moves as normal within the deck, but the cards are magickal windows into a different dimensional space. The occupant knows they are trapped in the deck, for its legend is well known, but from their point of view, they are in a room with no door and just a large aperture sealed by a magickal barrier. The only way in, or perhaps out, is through this window.

The meal comes, the meal goes. It isn't taken, it simply vanishes ... oh, why did I not ask to learn more?" She sobs, as she picks the dried blood from her hairline.

For her ex-majesty, all hope seems lost; she has pretty much forgotten the life she had before being imprisoned. Being seduced in such a manner, falling in love distracted her from duty and, as such, it all drifted from memory. Now, all she had was her role within the deck of cards ... The Queen of Hearts.

After a hard day in the deck, The Queen of Hearts, along with all the other occupants, was battered, beaten, and strewn across the table. The face of each card seemed to have a reddish-brown hue, so much so that each of the prisoners could barely be seen. It was the Head Jailor's job to inspect each card in each deck and ensure that the cards were not marked or damaged in any way—on the outside, at least.

The Jailor wearily turns each card face up and then using his hands, he gathers them all to the edge of the table One by one, he picks each card up, wipes it over with a cloth and places it neatly in a wooden box with the number 22 on its front in brass.

Deep down, he knew what was coming He had handled this deck thousands of times and had a hand in imprisoning some of the occupants, but none had he grown to have feelings for nor been intimate with—but one!

Her card was face down; he knew it was hers before he even realised what was happening. The Jailor, her tempter and seducer for his own wicked intent, was fearful for her life. He was actually suffering emotions for this woman he had schemed and devoted so much of his life, to exacting his revenge upon!

The Jailor ran his trembling hand over the card until his index finger found the edge, and then, with his thumb on the opposite edge, he paused before turning it gently over in his hand. There in his hands, through a blood-smeared barrier, was a broken figure of a fallen power: the Queen of the House of Hearts!

In his one moment of weakness, he slumps back into a chair and cries.

"Your Majesty, what have I done?"

A tear rolls down his cheek and off of his stubbled chin; it makes air-fall for a short time before splattering square in the middle of the card. In that one random moment of an emotive tear landing, the card's magick had been broken, and with what seemed like an electrical explosion the Queen of Hearts was free. Barely recognisable, with a build-up of dirt and a daily battering from within the deck, she stumbled as she stood. She was as surprised as the Jailor, who is sitting on the floor in amongst the remnants of a broken wooden chair.

The Jailor and The Queen took stock of the eerie silence and the sheer surprise at what had just happened—was she really free?

Was it as simple a solution as a tear from her convictor?

The thing is, no one ever knew. Soon after The Queen of The House of Hearts was convicted of unsanctioned coupling, the society she once stood for had rapidly changed. The great houses that ran everything were dissolved, and a council of trusted elders, one from each area of the known lands, formed a central government. The people revolted over their missing loved ones and, during a riot, all those who created the decks and knew their secrets perished in a fire. The House of Clubs was charged with looking after those remaining decks that were forever more prisons. Over time, and with a loss of hope for a way to free them, the cards were thought of as just that: a magickal deck of cards with moving pictures representing the cards' values. Only a few of the old guard knew what they were, but no others knew the secrets to escape. Just you and I.

The Head Jailor spoke first, but because of his shock, he just stuttered.

"I ... I ... I ... I am ..."

But then the Queen interrupted,

"You are what? SORRY? You ruined everything, and then you torment me daily by showing your face!"

She was, without a doubt, as angry as a viper and with every second that passed, the realisation that she was free increased her anger toward how she was betrayed. The Queen, with her usual grace and righteous purpose, grabs at a sheathed knife hung on the back of the door. Her movements flow as one, as she smoothly draws the knife and lunges at the Jailor's back!

With a shrill scream. the Jailor awoke—in his bed!

Every night his own guilt kills him, and every night he wakes up a victim, but is it really his mind making him pay for the acts he sought so freely to commit Himself to? Or is The Queen of Hearts playing the only game she can—reaching out through her own wicked devices?

THE REAL BOY
Scarlett Paige

"So, you want a *real* boy, do you? Bastard! Well, perhaps *you* need to be a **real** man first! Bastard!!"

Gepetto sidestepped to avoid yet another heavy, badly aimed trinket, and so it continued, with Blue screaming varying obscenities. All of them questioned Gepetto's age, libido, sexual prowess, and were punctuated with "I could've had a decent life," "I could've been someone," "Gave you the best years of my life!" And so on, and so forth, until Blue either ran out of trinkets to throw, or collapsed in a drunken, sobbing heap.

This night, it was the latter. Ironically, Gepetto had never actually said he wanted a 'real boy', but compared to Blue, and at this moment in time, it didn't seem such a bad idea. Real boy as opposed to crazy drunk, heroin-fuelled, over-emotional ladyboy with delusions of what could've been. It wasn't much of a contest!

"You didn't have any best years ... You daft junkie whore." Gepetto half-whispered as, for the 'who knows how many times?' He lifted Blue onto the bed, placed the duvet over her, and lit the remains of a half-smoked reefer.

There was no denying the fact that Blue was a mess, and so far down the line with drink and drugs that recovery seemed a distant, almost-forgotten idea. Despite the state of Blue, and the insane hopelessness of their situation, Gepetto loved Blue, and if he wanted anything, it was to turn the clock back and start again.

"I'm going out for a walk ... To clear my head ... I'll be back soon." he knew Blue couldn't hear him, but it was the most normal conversation they'd had all week.

Taking one final lungful of some pretty fine shit, Gepetto leant against the wall of his apartment block and watched the world go by. He had no idea how long he'd been stood there when a bad case of 'Mutton dressed as lamb' approached him.

"You look lonely darlin' ... What you say? I can show you a good time ... Why don't you come with me? I'll sort you out *real* good."

Her accent was a cross between the East End of Victorian London and the New York Bronx, and, in truth, he wasn't sure whether to laugh, run, or scream. He did neither. Instead, he looked her up and down; partially to make sure he wasn't dreaming, and partially because he was curious as to what she thought she could offer him.

"Well, darlin'," he said, doing his best to mimic her, whilst simultaneously regretting that last lungful, as the urge to giggle was becoming incredibly hard to control.

"Depends what you're offering." he knew that if she offered him her body, he wouldn't be able to stifle it any longer.

"A new club ... Pleasure Island ... 'Sonly just opened t'night ... First drink's on the 'owse ... Second one might be too ... If ya play yer cards right!" He shuddered at a wink that highlighted every last wrinkle and blemish on her face, which was almost as badly dressed as she was. "Let's face it love, ya look like ya could use a decent drink!"

She was right about that bit. He smiled and shrugged his shoulders, "Yeah go on then ... What the hell!!"

She took his hand and led him into the night. Gepetto had lived in Rome all his life, yet these streets were unfamiliar territory. He asked their location: where they were going? How much further? Questions of a similar nature were asked several times, but the answer was always either "You'll see" or a grin that, while it was meant to be friendly, possibly even cute, only made him wince. She seemed to get more and more unattractive with each smile, but he assumed that was probably the residual effects of the shit he'd smoked earlier. In between wincing and asking questions he even felt the odd pang of guilt, although he brushed it off, reminding himself he was only going for a drink and that Blue would be out cold for hours yet.

As for the somewhat grotesque creature that was still leading him by the hand, he couldn't decide whether she was his captor or saviour but thought it might be advisable to ask her name. Especially as it was dark, and he had no idea where the hell he was.

"So, I take it you have a name?"

"They call me *Honesty* darlin'."

He couldn't help but snigger, '*Honesty?* ... *Really?*' She hadn't been anything other than completely evasive.

"Well Honesty, we've walking for ages, and it seems a long old trek for one fucking drink. It better be *one hell* of a club."

"It is ... honestly ... With a name like Honesty, I wouldn't lie now ... Would I?"

Gepetto sighed. He was becoming resigned to the fact that it was obviously miles away, and that *Honesty* wasn't about to give him any real answers. Plus, he had no idea how to get home, so he would just have to wait till he got there and saw for himself. Truth to tell, his lack of knowledge regarding his current location was very unnerving, if not frightening, but being male, he wasn't about to admit that. He tried to ignore the images racing through his head of 'snuff movies' and 'gang rape.' In his mid-thirties, surely, he was a little old for the sex trade.

His head was still buzzing from trying to ignore the voices of reason and panic, when Honesty's grating voice cut in ...

"We're here ... In ya go, 'n' tell 'em Honesty sent ya ..."

He wasn't really certain which was worse: the pseudo-London/New York/Bronx streetwalker accent, or the hideously distorted grimace of her wink. But by God, he needed a drink!!

"Oops, nearly forgot," she added, stamping his hand before shoving him through the open door.

It was hard to tell how busy it was, because once inside it was thick with smoke, and rang with the sound of laughter and dance music. What looked like shadows, but he assumed were people, moved gracefully around the room. He squinted at the back of his hand, trying to make out what was written, but it was impossible to see in the dim light of the club. Eventually, he reached the bar and was handed a drink by a very beautiful young man, with dark curly hair and a *very* well-toned physique.

Gepetto guessed at him being in his early twenties, and over the next couple of drinks he discovered they called him 'Pinocchio.'

"Like the puppet??" Gepetto quizzed, smiling at the irony of it all.

"Yes, just like the puppet ... and mostly it's 'Nocchio."

"Is that your real name?"

"Nah! They call me it on account of how flexible I am, "he responded, by flipping onto the bar and doing the splits. "See ... I got no strings!"

He moved so quickly that Gepetto scarcely had time to grab his drink before the beautiful young man was groin to bar in front of him. And Gepetto may well have been still reeling from the night's events, but he was not a celibate monk and would've had to be blind not to notice the bulge on the bar staring him in the face.

There was nothing subtle about Gepetto's expression as he felt the lust within him. It was the sort of inevitable lust that began slowly but burned as it rose to an all-consuming frenzy. He bit his lower lip, unable to control it any longer. The man slammed his legs shut and jumped down, beaming. Gepetto scarcely noticed, he was too busy struggling with his own thoughts. The man placed his hand on Gepetto's groin; the bulge was evident, even through his jeans, and growing by the second.

'Yes! Yes! I *do* want a real boy' was the only coherent thought Gepetto had as he stood up. He slammed Nocchio against the wall and kissed him more passionately than he had kissed anyone in a long time, his tongue probing deeply.

Nocchio responded by gently pulling away and kissing, biting, and licking Gepetto's neck. He worked his was slowly down his body, savouring every moment, teasing his nipples and lingering slightly, before running his tongue slowly across the tip of his shining manhood. Both men were oblivious to their surroundings; the smoky haze, shadowy figures, and music faded into the background, and Nocchio could taste the Gepetto's excitement rising with every flick of his tongue. His own cock, too, was growing increasingly uncomfortable by the second. He deftly undid his own trousers, which had been struggling to contain him, and worked his way back up to kiss Gepetto with their swollen cocks pressing against each other.

"Fuck me" Nocchio whispered.

Gepetto didn't need telling twice. He flipped Nocchio round, and took him there and then, up against the bar. He hadn't done anything like that since his youth, and his cock throbbed while Nocchio wriggled with pleasure, as he worked it in and out, until he could no longer contain it. His body shuddered as the warm, sticky cum seemed to spurt endlessly. He pulled away, allowing Nocchio to turn around, his own cock in his hand. He pulled it back, ejaculating over Gepetto's still hard manhood, before dropping to his knees and drinking his fill.

This time he worked Gepetto: probing his prick with his tongue, swallowing the full length, cupping and licking his balls alternately. There seemed no end to this erotic bliss as Gepetto dropped to his hands and knees, begging to be fucked. He knew nothing about this man, other than that he was a flexible, unparalleled lover. Nor did he know where he was, and nor did he care; more importantly, he had forgotten all about Blue with her nasty taunts and continual drug and alcohol abuse. Tonight, he was free!

He didn't know how long the night lasted, he just knew that he didn't want it to end, but, like all good nights, it *did* eventually end and Gepetto woke up slumped in a doorway in a street not far from home. He blinked at the morning sun and rubbed his eyes with his palms, trying to take stock of his current situation. He didn't remember very much on waking, hazy fragments that gradually grew more vivid as he became fully awake. He felt calmer than he had ever felt, and a smile crawled over his face as he remembered Nocchio and their night of passion, wincing slightly at the fact that it had all taken place in a busy nightclub. What if someone had seen him, either being led by the hand of some dodgy old tart, or, worse still, shafting Nocchio up against the wall.

Apart from anything else, and regardless of the drugs, it all seemed very out of character; maybe it was all just a dream. After all, sex was never that good and, though there are many beautiful young men out there, few are *that* exceptional. He concluded it *must* have been a just that—a dream, brought about as a result of some exceptionally good dope, coupled with his turbulent, if not hopeless, life with Blue.

'Gods! Blue!' The thought entered his mind like a sledgehammer and his heart raced. She would have woken up by now and be frantic with anger and worry. He looked at his watch and there, on the back of his hand, staring back at him in bold capital letters was the word 'REMEMBER.' Although it was slightly smudged, it was still legible.

Slowly he got up, a host of thoughts racing through his mind as he pieced together his evening with Nocchio. He walked home trying to remember every little detail of the previous night but was constantly distracted by the angry expression, he envisioned Blue would be wearing. Eventually, he arrived at their apartment to discover he was more or less right about Blue's expression.

She was desperately trying to organise her gear and works: teaspoon in one hand, lighter in the other, and shaking with both withdrawal and anger. "So! You're back?" she snarled, through her clenched teeth. "And is there any point to asking where you've been? ... Or who with?"

Gepetto sighed, gently taking the paraphernalia. "Let me."

He prepared her fix as she continued her tirade.

"Well ...Who was he?? Hope it was worth it! So, this is how you repay my love!!..." And so on.

She was still mumbling about how he had ruined her life, broken her heart, and, of course, how she could have been somebody, and so on, as he inserted the needle between her toes. Blue's veins were a thing of the past. She had been so busy ranting at him that she hadn't noticed how much heroin Gepetto had used, and Gepetto, who hadn't listened to his conscience in the last 12 hours, saw no reason to start now. He knew he would never return to that club, or ever meet Nocchio or the strange old woman again but, equally, he couldn't continue this life any longer and nor could Blue.

As Blue slipped into unconsciousness, with her works beside her on the bed, Gepetto closed the door of their apartment behind him, knowing that as her life was ending his was just beginning. This time he was going to follow his heart ...

And hell yes! He wanted a real boy!!

PRIDE

PRIDE
Diane Narraway

It always comes
Before a fall.
That supercilious,
Egotistical call
Of one who believes
They're better than most,
And feels compelled
To gloat and boast.
Yet beneath the arrogance,
All can see
Just how foolish
Pride can be,
And the bigger the ego,
The harder the fall.
It's a long harsh drop
From walking tall,
But there's no need
To take that tumble.
Just try and be,
A bit more humble.

THE SWAN SONG OF TWO SISTERS
Jennie Jones

"Fuck me ... what is this muck?"

The carer faltered,

"Excuse me? We don't use language like that here."

"I wouldn't feed this to a dog," exclaimed Priscilla, "I might be old, but I'm not stupid."

She prodded the contents of her bowl. Chunks of meat, potato, and vegetables bobbed around in the gravy. Humaira glanced over at her older sister's lunch, it did look pretty rough.

"Shush," she urged, "Please don't make a scene. Not on our first morning here."

But Priscilla wouldn't be silenced.

"It looks like the contents of a cesspit," she announced.

A hush fell over the dining-hall.

"Everyone is looking at us," said Humaira.

"Good," said Priscilla, turning back to the carer. "Bring me something else. Quick smart, before I get you sacked."

The other residents looked over, craning to hear—something that was becoming increasingly difficult with their advanced ages.

The gossip would start, probably before the sisters were even out of earshot. What first impression had the newcomers given? What would they be like, to live with? What were their health complaints? Estimated time left?

The carer cleared her throat, "Madam ..."

"Don't 'madam' me," said Priscilla, "Just do it. Do you know who I am? I am Priscilla."

The carer, a young woman in her 20s, shuffled uncomfortably. She wasn't paid enough to put up with such grief. And no, she didn't know who the woman was, and neither did she care. She shook her head.

"Oh, for fuck's sake. I'm Priscilla ... PRISCILLA ... of the FOUR FONTANELLES."

Humaira looked up; time to run through the spiel again.

"Priscilla was a famous jazz singer, back in the 50s. Household name. Famous recording artist. Toured the world. I was her manager."

Priscilla smiled, proudly.

"Don't worry darling," she said, "it wasn't your fault for not knowing. Someone should have told you who I was before I arrived."

But the carer wasn't listening. She'd taken the bowl and walked off. Humaira turned to her sister.

"Darling, you didn't need to be so nasty," she said.

"Oh, you're too soft," said Priscilla, "I don't know what you'd do without me. Now, pass me my make-up bag; I need a touch up. I hope you remembered it."

Humaira dug out the required lipstick. Barely midday, and her sister already had a full face of slap. With it, she wore a flowing velvet dress and black sequinned slippers. A very different look to her own hand-knitted cardigan and flowery smock.

The pair watched through the windows, as a removals van pulled up outside. A man jumped out and spoke to the receptionist. Then he pulled the van door open and started to unload boxes.

"Ooh, look; it's our things," remarked Humaira.

"About time too," said Priscilla, 'Should have been here yesterday.'

Out came the cardboard boxes that Humaira had packed the previous week; the boxes full of memorabilia of their previous lives. Boxes of trinkets, of gifts given by adoring fans, a cushion hand-sewn by a royal child, photos, and newspaper cuttings of Priscilla's illustrious career.

And then came the suitcases: three large suitcases for Priscilla, stuffed full of frocks, evening gowns, and accessories; and one suitcase for Humaira, and her knitting bag.

Another plate of food arrived: ham sandwiches, with a side-salad and a bag of crisps. Priscilla pushed it aside.

She reached for her mobile phone and turned it on. No messages. She frowned. Why no messages? There used to be a lot of messages.

Another carer came over; a slightly older, bouncy woman, with a clipboard.
"We don't normally allow mobile phones in communal areas. Could I ask you to put it away?"
"What?" growled Priscilla. "Do you know who you are talking to?"
Blank face. Priscilla's face hardened.
"Please don't," begged Humaira, "They're all too young."
Priscilla huffed, "What is it with today's youth? No idea about quality music."
"I've got a degree in music," said the carer. "I come in one day a week to run a music and movement class. Maybe you'd like to join us? At 2pm, in the living room?"
"That sounds like fun," said Humaira.
"No, it doesn't," said Priscilla. "Not for us. We've got things to do."
"Oh, the unpacking? We can help you with that."
"No thanks. We can manage."
"Well, if you change your minds …"
Priscilla hoisted herself up. Getting older was no fun. What was she now? 85? 86? And her sister—three years younger?

She took her walking stick and directed her sister to follow her back to their room. A shared twin room: two beds, side-by-side, such as the room they'd once shared as girls. Before her career had taken off. When she'd still been somebody. When she'd still had money.

Now she was in a foul mood.

"Come on," she hissed.

And the two of them shuffled back to their room.

Inside, they found a neat pile of boxes and suitcases. Humaira started to open them, as Priscilla watched.

"It's hard work, Priscilla," she complained, sitting down, out of breath.

"You're useless. Why don't you take one of your heart pills, or whatever it is you need?" said Priscilla. "We're only here because of you. I don't need to be here."

"That's mean," said Humaira.

"But true," said Priscilla. "I suppose I'd better unpack, then. Right. Now, this is your stuff; keep it out of my way."

Priscilla nudged a red hatbox under Humaira's bed. She'd seen it before; it was full of papers, and photos, and whatnot ... crap that her sister kept.

"And my stuff ..." she said. Her attention was already back on her own cases.

Priscilla started to unpack her clothes. She unfolded each item one-by-one, and lovingly inspected it before hanging it in the wardrobe.

"They'll need ironing," she commented, "We'll need a girl to come in, to do that."

The wardrobe filled quickly, as did her sister's wardrobe.

"Tut, tut ... not enough room," said Priscilla. "You don't need much space, Humaira. You've always travelled light, and your clothes aren't as delicate as mine. Will you be all right with the chest of drawers?"

She turned round. Her sister had leaned back into her chair, eyes shut.

How did they get so old? If Priscilla was honest with herself, she was a little past her prime herself. Her hands were wrinkled and shaky and she wasn't as fast on her feet as she used to be. She felt tired too, but she couldn't let on to the outside world—she had a reputation, an image, to maintain.

Her thoughts were broken by the ringing of her phone. At last ... she was expecting their call.

"Miss Priscilla?"

"Yes." Her voice cracked. How annoying.

"I'm a producer for the TV show, 'Celebrity Secrets'. You've been expecting our call?"

"Yes, of course."

They wanted to interview her sister; Priscilla had already filmed her interview, several weeks before. She wasn't sure if she wanted to be on the show. The idea behind it, was for a panel of highly competent former detectives to grill celebrities, to extract their secrets.

Like everyone else, she had her secrets; and she didn't want them exposed. But it had been years since she'd been on TV, and 'Celebrity Secrets' was prime time viewing. The lure was too strong.

Predictably, she'd been tight-lipped on her grilling. But now it would be time for her entourage, in this case her sister, to be put under the spotlight. What gems could be gleaned from her younger sibling?

Priscilla had considered this. The program makers were like hungry animals. She could surely dig out some titbits to satisfy them. Maybe the story of how Priscilla stole Humaira's beau, when they were young girls? Or the time that Priscilla was ill, so she dressed Humaira up to look like her, to sign autographs in a shopping mall. That kind of thing.

"We'll come to you," said the voice on the phone. "We know you've just moved into a nursing home. We've spoken to the staff and they're happy for us to film in a spare room. It won't take long."

"And me?"

"Just your sister, I'm afraid. That's part of the show: to get her alone. But don't worry, we'll take good care of her."

The woman hung up. Priscilla put the phone on the table and turned back to her sister.

"Humaira, wake up. We've got work to do."

A strong cup of coffee was acquired, and Humaira was prodded back into life.

They spent the afternoon rehearsing for the interview. It was important that Humaira didn't mess up. This could be Priscilla's last big moment on television. The nation that once loved her so much, now seemed to have forgotten about her.

Priscilla arranged their chairs, so they were facing each other. She also turned on the angle-poise lamp, so it was shining in Humaira's face. Humaira squirmed uncomfortably.

"Must you put the light there?"
"Yes."

And over the next few hours, Priscilla ran through their lives together. About how neither sister had married, although Priscilla had had plenty of suitors. About the five award-winning albums that Priscilla had released. About how Humaira had always been behind the scenes, taking care of the more mundane side of things.

Truth be told, she couldn't have done all this without Humaira; not that she'd admit it to her. She could barely admit it to herself, but deep down, Humaira's contribution had been invaluable. A contribution that the world didn't need to know about.

"Humaira," said Priscilla. "Look at me. This one is important."

The coffee was wearing off, and Humaira was becoming sluggish.

"Remember that time when we were girls, and you came into the recording studio?"

"Oh yes," Humaira's eyes lit up. "We did that a lot."

"Well, once or twice maybe. For backing vocals."

"Backing vocals? What about that song I wrote? It was called ... er ... I thought I sang the main part. It was our little secret."

Damn. Her sister couldn't remember what she'd eaten for lunch, or even if she'd had lunch, but she could remember 70 years as clear as day.

"No, we didn't record that; you must be mistaken."

"Oh, I thought we did."

"No, so you don't need to mention any of that to the producers tomorrow, do you?"

"Um ... what's happening tomorrow?"

Priscilla leaned back in her chair. This wasn't going to work; it would be a disaster.

As the evening came, she tried again, but her sister became more and more confused, and then upset.

Dinner came and went: rice and chicken. Good. Couldn't go wrong there, even though

Humaira would have preferred something more elaborate.

More coaching. More requests to meet the residents, do a jigsaw, take tea in the conservatory ... and so on. Priscilla batted back all invitations, asking that time be given for them to settle in first.

And the day drew to a close. Her younger sister sat looking at her, awaiting more instructions, but nothing was sticking. She couldn't allow her sister to be interviewed.

Priscilla felt anger welling up in her.

"Why are you so useless?" she hissed.

"I'm sorry," Humaira gulped.

Priscilla's fists started to clench. It had been a long time since she'd hit her sister. It wasn't even easy to clench her fists these days, but the frustration became too much for her.

Priscilla started to club Humaira around the ears.

"Why. Are. You. So. Stupid?" She timed her words with the punches.

Humaira started to cry.

"Please stop. You're hurting me."

And it felt like they were children again; as in some ways, they were. Always sisters, always fighting like sisters, like the children they'd once been.

Only Humaira didn't bounce back so easily now. She flopped back into her chair, clutching her chest and gasping. Then nothing.

Priscilla didn't notice at first. She'd given up punching Humaira, and was now punching Humaira's pillow, but then she turned back to Humaira.

"Oh for God's sake, surely you've not gone back to sleep? I was only talking to you seconds ago. Well, you can just stay there. Serves you right."

Priscilla climbed into her nightdress and went through the usual pre-bedtime routine of removing her make-up, putting her hair in a net, and putting her false teeth into a jar. After setting her alarm, she turned off the light and went to sleep.

When morning came, Priscilla woke up just before the alarm went off at 7am.

The solution had come to her: she would take Humaira's place. Granted, she'd have to wear one of her sister's drab smocks and a terrible cardigan. She'd have to forgo the make-up too, but they'd always looked very similar; even more-so now they were old, with grey hair and wrinkles that had layered their once good looks.

Priscilla got up and opened the curtains. Now she could see what she was doing.

She picked out some of her sister's clothes and put them on. She found her sister's shoes, by the side of the bed and put them on too; then she went to look for her sister's glasses.

Odd: she normally keep them by the side of her bed. Also odd, her sister wasn't in her bed; it didn't appear to have been slept in.

She looked around the room. Her sister was still in the chair, asleep and still wearing her glasses.

Priscilla reached over to take the glasses. Maybe she could remove them without waking her sister. She really could do without all the questions ... without the "Why are you going without me?"

She removed the glasses easily. Too easily. Priscilla looked closer; was her sister breathing? She seemed very still. Very quiet.

She prodded Humaira.

"Humaira? Humaira? Wake up."

No response. What to do? Priscilla thought fast. He sister was obviously dead, or if not quite dead, almost dead. Same thing really.

She could raise the alarm, but that would mean the show wouldn't be filmed. They'd know it wasn't her sister.

Or ... she could raise the alarm later. Rush through the filming, and then deal with her sister. Plan B was the way to go.

But there were some modifications to the plan. She couldn't risk suspicion, or even concern, over a resident not showing up for breakfast, but there was a way around this. She still had plenty of time; the camera crew wasn't due to arrive until 10am.

Priscilla quickly re-dressed, as herself. She pulled on a suitable dress and shawl, and threw her make-up on, as the seasoned pro she was. Then she made her way to the breakfast hall.

Good. It was still so early, hardly anyone else was up. She was greeted by a carer, who ticked off her name as she made her way to a table.

"Where's your sister?" asked the attendant.

"She'll be down soon," said Priscilla, "she's just getting herself up."

"Does she need any help?"

"No, no, she's fine."

Priscilla ordered her breakfast: toast and jam would suffice, and a pot of tea. She wolfed it down, as quick as she could, and returned to her room.

Her sister was in the same position. She really was dead. Priscilla would deal with that later.

Off came the posh dress and shawl. She wiped the makeup off her face, then climbed back into her sister's clothes, complete with glasses.

Time for breakfast number two, so down she went. Back to the breakfast hall, where she had her sister's name ticked off the register, and enjoyed yet more toast, and another pot of tea.

Already, it was 10am and the TV crew had already arrived. They had placed an armchair next to a window and set up a lighting rig around it.

The cast members trickled in. There were four of them: two men and two women; all highly eminent in their fields of psychology, detective work, and the like. One by one, they would be filmed sitting with her, probing her for secrets.

As the pro she was, Priscilla fed them what they wanted. She told them the stories she had rehearsed with her sister, about the shenanigans of their youth: the lovers, the parties, the decadence of the 1970s. They lapped it up.

And as another testament to her professionalism, she tried to be nice: she smiled at the crew. She looked down, and adopted a humble, shy, demeanour. She spoke softly, like a woman who didn't care if the world didn't notice her—a woman like her sister. It was fun, this acting lark, even if the character was a bit wet.

The hour allocated by the care home was up. The staff nurse came in, commenting about Humaira's (or Priscilla's) advanced years, and also pointing out that Humaira had not yet received her daily medication.

In front of the television crew, the nurse kneeled down in front of Priscilla, and emptied three small white pills into a bowl. She also handed her a glass of water.

"I'm so sorry we didn't give these to you earlier," she said.

Priscilla looked at the pills: small, white, and inoffensive. They weren't the pills she was on; she'd already been given her pills that morning. Could they hurt her, as they weren't hers?

The crew looked at her, everyone looked at her. She couldn't refuse them, not without revealing her true identity. She had no choice. One by one, she popped the tablets in her mouth, and swallowed them.

"So, are we finished?" she asked the crew.

"Yes. Though maybe we could have a quick word with Priscilla if she's around?"

"Shall I go and get her?" asked the nurse.

"No."

The word came out more forcefully than Priscilla meant it to and certainly louder than the tone Humaira would have used.

"I'm sorry; I mean, it's best I get her," she said. "Help her put her make-up on. She likes to look her best."

Of course, everyone nodded. Priscilla stood up to go. Odd, she felt dizzy; she must have stood up too fast.

She bid her farewells and headed back to her room.

She definitely felt dizzy. Gosh, it must be those tablets. The walk back to her room felt longer than ever. She opened the door and let herself in.

Good. No one had been in. The room, and her sister, were just as she'd left them.

But what was that, on the bed? The hatbox belonging to her sister. It was open. She went over, for a closer look.

Inside, were photos and press releases from the olden days. She pulled some of them out. How lovely. She'd have a closer look at these later.

And underneath, what were these? They looked like diaries, dating from the 1950s, when she'd first become a teenage singing sensation, through to the modern era. She flicked through. The last entry had been yesterday: her younger sister had written about the coaching session, about how she wanted to say the right thing, and how Priscilla thought she was so dumb, but she wasn't dumb.

"I could sing," the entry continued, "I sang on Priscilla's records. I wrote songs. She won't let me talk about it. I must remember not to."

More diaries. The earlier ones written so long ago, were full of song lyrics, songs in progress, details of recording sessions. The sessions that had recorded the vocals that had launched Priscilla to stardom. But not her sister—the true singer on the records.

"Your voice was wasted on you," hissed Priscilla, turning to her dead sister's body, "I had the looks ... the charisma ... the personality..."

The room was starting to spin. Priscilla was beginning to feel most unwell. She reached out, to nothing in particular, to try to steady herself, but felt herself falling. She should be getting dressed, getting ready to go back out as herself—as Priscilla, the worldwide singing sensation.

But already, she knew the secret was out. It wouldn't be long before the nurses, and then the TV crew, came knocking on her door. The truth would be discovered, and the world would know what a sham she really was.

SIN AND BONE
Kathy Sharp

Once upon a time there was a collector of animals. He travelled far to the jungles of South America, taking bottles, bags, and a gun with him. Soon, he had filled the bags with the preserved skins and bones of the animals he had shot, and he had pickled many smaller animals, insects, and fishes in spirits of wine. All of it was ready to take home: he had a great study of natural history, an exhibition of specimens, and a wonderful book planned. But he had not yet encountered a sloth; it was a vital part of the collection, he thought. He could not return without one, so he searched on.

One morning, to his delight, he opened his eyes and there, in the tree above him, was a sloth. He reached for his gun.

'Stop,' said the sloth.

'Eh?' said the collector.

'Stop, I say. It is very poor form to shoot an unarmed opponent, is it not?'

The collector had to agree: it was bad form.

'I hadn't considered it before,' he said.

'Time you did,' said the sloth, swaying languidly on its branch.

'Shocking laziness, sir.'

'That's rich, coming from something named "sloth",' said the collector, 'and it's a deadly sin, to boot.'

'Stuff and nonsense,' said the sloth, waving a hooked claw, 'besides, that is just your opinion. We consider the practice of taking your time to be a great virtue, I'll have you know, and no kind of deadly sin at all.'

'That's as may be,' said the collector, reaching for his gun again, 'but I need your skin and bones for my collection. It will confer a kind of immortality upon you, after all. Why, the king himself might look at you.'

'Tempting,' said the sloth, dangling by two legs only, 'but I think not. And my objection to shooting unarmed opponents still stands. You are a gentleman, are you not?'

The collector considered it; he was a gentleman. 'Well,' he said, 'now that I've made your acquaintance, it does seem a little unsporting. Suppose I give you a head start?'

'You cannot be serious,' said the sloth, becoming so indignant it almost fell off its branch. 'I am not one of your running-about-in-haste creatures. It would be no advantage at all.'

'Enough of this nonsense,' said the collector, taking aim, 'I shall shoot you anyway. It is an affront to my pride as a gentleman to be bandying words with a sloth.'

'No matter, sir,' said the sloth, quite unconcerned, 'I have kept you talking just long enough, I see. Look downward, do.'

The collector looked down. Trooping across his boots and about to march on up his trouser leg was a brigade of soldier ants, with snapping jaws. In no time they had felled him, and soon there was nothing left, nothing left of him but skin and bone.

The sloth watched. 'Pride goeth before a fall,' it said, being a particularly well-read creature, 'and that is a deadly sin too, I believe. Particularly in your case, sir.' And it went slowly on its way.

COWBOY PIE
Fi Woods

Nigel sat with his eyes closed, in his recliner, turning his Stetson around in his hands as he pondered. He was trying to find les mots justes; he knew that he had what he needed in his head, but it was eluding him. He groaned as he heard the key scraping in the door, 'That's her back then,' he quietly said to himself, 'I'm not going to be able to get this finished now, not with all of her brouhaha. She'll insist on chatting and the two of us "spending quality time together," why can't she understand that I just want to be left in peace?' He put the Stetson back on his head and moved his laptop to the side-table just as the door banged back and Kate tried to edge her way through the opening with several bags of shopping. Nigel sighed to himself and plastered a smile on his face.

'Nige, grab the rest of the shopping out of the car would you?'

'Get the boys to do it; it won't hurt them to start helping out a bit.'

'They keep their room tidy, and they put their dirty clothes in the laundry basket; I think that's good enough for their age. You're really expecting them to be able to carry heavy, full, bags of shopping? Without all the groceries ending up on the pavement? I struggled with the bags I brought in, and those are the lightest. It won't hurt you to pull your weight a bit more.'

'I have neither time nor the room in my head to carry out household jobs, my dear. I need to relax and allow my thoughts to wander where they will.'

Nigel was a hefty, jowly, corpulent man who had taught English at the local comprehensive. He retired at 40 to write a book, despite the fact that even his short stories had been rejected by all and sundry. He recalled that a number of authors had a certain something that was necessary for them to be able to write. For himself it was a Stetson: his writing hat. As well as confirming his status as an author, it reinforced his masculinity when Kate demeaned him for not providing any income, and it signified his future as man of riches and power.

His wife was as thin as a rake. She had continued her childhood ballet lessons at The Royal Ballet School after obtaining a scholarship at the age of 7. She'd danced professionally for many years, working her way from the corps de ballet to principal dancer. After retiring at 35, she'd taken the self-employed teaching route, so common to retired ballerinas and opened her own dance school. She enjoyed the fact that she could make her work fit in with her life but was becoming ever more annoyed at being the sole earner. Regardless of what Nigel said about writing, the fact was that while she worked he simply sat in a chair.

The boys were identical twins, aged five. Exuberant and noisy though they were, they seldom squabbled, seeming to enjoy each other's company. They both had the same hint-of-ginger dark blond hair, the same spray of freckles across the nose, and the same seemingly constant smile and infectious giggles. There was one immediate benefit to having two children at the same time: there was no need for arguments over a name; they each named one baby. Kate chose Nikolai, after her principal dancer partner, and Nigel chose Holden, in homage to J.D Salinger. Kate flatly refused this and insisted that Nigel choose something else. He picked Aleksandr, inspired by Solzhenitsyn, and Kate found this perfectly acceptable.

Since leaving teaching Nige had sent a steady stream of novels to various publishers and received an equally steady stream of rejections. Nonetheless, he remained convinced of his literary brilliance and with each knockback he bellowed at Kate,

'Heathens, one and all. They publish trash and can't recognise true talent when it's in front of them.' Kate had tried suggesting that publishers probably knew their business pretty well, but that only incurred a tantrum and a period of sulking.

'Even you doubt me, do you? My own wife. Where is your loyalty, your support, your encouragement?' When Kate pointed out that she was supporting the household it didn't improve matters one iota.

'Is it not right for a wife to support her husband? You try to make me feel guilty by claiming that you do everything while I don't contribute. Do you think your attitude helps? How am I supposed to write when you are constantly demeaning me?'

'I feel like a single parent Nige. You don't show any interest in the boys; you never come to watch them in the things they do and the only words you ever say to them are 'Be quiet.' We all want, and need, your attention and love. It can't go on like this.'

'Can you please be patient Kate? None of the great artists received their due recognition straight away. I promise you that the book I'm working on now will definitely be accepted for publication. It's the absolute best thing I've ever done. And then, after publication the film rights ... This is going to make us rich; we'll buy a bigger house and you'll be able to stop working. We'll be able to have holidays ... whatever you want.'

Kate sighed and said to herself 'I just want my husband back' but out loud said 'Ok Nige. Go for it.'

Life continued, for all of them, exactly the same for another six months. Well, not quite exactly the same: with Nigel refusing to interact at all with his family, Kate and the twins gradually became more and more detached from him. There was no feeling of unity or togetherness; it was three people living one life, while another enjoyed a completely different, and separate, existence.

Kate arrived home one Friday, the boys were having a sleepover with a friend, and much to her surprise Nigel wasn't tapping away on his laptop. He looked up from the newspaper he was reading and smiled at her. Standing up from his chair, he said 'Come here darling.' Kate hesitantly walked towards him and found herself enveloped in his arms. She couldn't even remember the last time he'd shown her any affection; it felt like a complete stranger was touching her.

'Sit down love; you look shattered. I'll get us a drink.' Kate kicked her shoes off and curled into her corner of the sofa. She watched Nigel get out the keep-for-best glasses and his precious Tanqueray No. Ten gin. He had quite a collection, considering himself something of a connoisseur. 'Who is this man?' Kate said to herself. 'He can't possibly be my husband. Something very strange has happened here.' Nigel handed one of the glasses to Kate and said, 'A toast, my dear, to the future.' They clinked glasses and for the first time in years Nigel eschewed his recliner to sit in the other corner of the sofa, opposite his wife.

'You seem happy Nige; what are we celebrating?'

'The most thrilling story has been told, I finished my book and have sent it to several publishers. There's no doubt that this one will be accepted; it's jampacked full of excitement and intrigue, and the characters are diverse and engaging. I gave this one my all; I put my heart and soul into it. I have actually written a book far better than I'd ever thought possible. If this one gets rejected, I'll eat my hat.'

'It sounds really good Nige and I love seeing you being so positive. As much as I don't want to pour cold water on this moment of achievement and success, I have to tell you Nige that if this one is turned down and you do not return to a full-time job, the boys and I will be gone.'

'It's been hard for you sweetheart, I know that, but don't worry; we're heading into Easy Street now.' Behind his smile Nige's head was thinking, 'There ain't a chance in hell. She'll never leave me. Where would she go? And it's a moot point anyway; this one not being published is about as likely to happen as the American public boycotting McDonalds.'

Days came and went with Kate asking Nigel, 'Any news?' each time she arrived home. The answer was always negative, but with a positive spin, 'No, not yet Kate, but these things take time.' Kate began bringing home the local newspaper regularly, for the "situations vacant" pages. Nigel took them and resentfully put them to the side.

'You're jumping the gun somewhat Kate. Have faith.'

A further three months passed during which Nigel had again begun tapping on his laptop.

'A sequel,' he explained.

'Now who's jumping the gun?' asked Kate.

One day Nigel decided that he'd surprise Kate (and sweeten her up) by having dinner ready when she and the twins arrived home. He was actually quite a good cook, when he could be bothered, so he prepared his wife's favourite: lasagne and garlic bread.

As her usual arrival time approached, he took a bottle of white wine from the fridge and set the table ready. He took the food from the oven and covered it with foil to keep it warm. Looking up at the kitchen clock he realised that he'd been so preoccupied that he hadn't noticed they were 15 minutes late. 'Probably traffic,' he thought. When they hadn't arrived after half an hour he tried to call Kate, but her phone went to voicemail.

The garlic bread became hard, the lasagne congealed, and Nigel was still waiting for his family to come home to him. As he stood at the living room window looking out for them, he confidently decided, 'I'm sure there's an explanation; something has delayed her,'

He poured himself a glass of the wine and relaxed with his laptop and Stetson. 'Silver linings and all that; I've got peace and quiet a-plenty.'

The clock ticked the time away and after a couple of hours Nigel called the police to report them as missing.

'She's an adult sir, and we don't start looking for people until at least 24 hours have passed.' 'But the children ...' 'They are with their mother, who is an adult sir. You need to allow at least 24 hours.' Nigel slammed the phone in disgust and frustration and decided he'd have to find them and bring them home himself.

He rang the local hospitals, but none of them had any record of his wife or the boys. Then it occurred to him to look in the bedrooms; at first glance it all appeared normal: the beds were made, and the rooms were tidy.

'Nothing to worry about; they'll be here any minute,' he said as he went back down the stairs.

He'd just sat down to continue working on his sequel when a thought occurred to him: he hadn't checked the wardrobes and chests of drawers.

'Might as well do the job properly,' he grumbled and went back up the stairs, Stetson still in place. First he checked Kate's wardrobe and noticed immediately that a lot of her clothing was missing; it was the same when he looked in the boys' drawers.

'Ah, now I understand; she's gone to her mother's.' Nigel picked up the extension in the master bedroom and dialled.

'Abbi, it's Nigel. Are Kate, Nikolai, and Aleksandr with you?'

'Hello Nigel,' came the cool reply. Abbi had been far from impressed with Nigel when he stopped supporting the family.

'No, they're not here. They came round earlier for dinner and Kate said they were going on holiday.'

'Holiday? What do you mean? Where? For how long?'

'I have no idea, Nigel; I assumed that you knew all about it. She said that they all needed some fun and relaxation and you needed peace to write. After we'd eaten she called a taxi for the airport, said that she'd be in touch, and off they went.'

'I can't believe that she'd just up and away without telling me.'

'Well I'm sorry Nigel, there's nothing else I can tell you.'

Nigel hung up and shrugged, 'I'm sure that giving me the time and peace to write was meant to be a nice surprise.' He went back to the kitchen, poured some more wine, and took it into the living room. He got comfortable in his recliner, settled his Stetson more firmly into place, and turned his attention back to his laptop.

He'd written a couple of paragraphs when he realised that something about Kate was niggling at him. What was it? Something she'd done? No, not something she'd done; it was something she'd said, but what? 'It couldn't have been anything important, or I'd remember it,' he muttered as he continued to type. Mid-sentence her voice came back to him: she'd said that she'd take the boys and go.

'She'll be back; this is her home and her life, and I'm her husband.' Nigel continued to write until he was tired and ready for bed. He stretched out blissfully in the half-empty bed and fell asleep secure in the knowledge that in the morning all would be returned to normal.

He slept well and woke late, surprised that the house was still silent. Downstairs the flashing red light of the answerphone caught his eye.

'Hello Nigel. You are now utterly free to write without any distraction. Goodbye.'

Nigel sat at the kitchen table with a mug of tea, and placed his Stetson next to it ...

THE IRIZINIUM PRIESTESS
Moira Hodgkinson

In a room filled with silk, velvet, glittering jewels, fine draperies, and the soft amber glow of thirteen candles, Lady Solivante prepared herself.

She perfumed and polished herself, glued long lashes in place to frame crimson-coloured eyes, pinned up the silver and copper tresses of her curling hair, and allowed her aides fasten the laces in the back of her corset. Her gilt-tinged arms were no longer flexible enough to reach back and do this task herself. She examined her reflection in a gilt-edged mirror. The corset would come off again soon enough, but she insisted on refinement for her clients.

'I'm ready.' she said, with no trace of eagerness and Martin and Monrose withdrew. She was still uncertain if they were brothers or lovers, but she was grateful that they had remained her faithful servants over the long years. After a moment, her guest walked in, still holding the glass of chilled Champagne he had been presented with upon his arrival.

Elegantly long steel fingernails whispered against layers of satin and taffeta as Lady Solivante hitched her skirts up, giving a hint of promises ahead. Eric looked terrified and she feared he would crush the delicate glass he held in his hand.

'Don't be scared.' Lady Solivante whispered. 'This is what you paid for, after all. To experience my ... difference.'

Eric was a remarkably common name for one who came, she'd been assured, from a tremendously wealthy, noble family. Certainly, his credentials had been deemed in order by her aides. Martin and Monrose were careful and thorough in that respect; she would never think to question their judgement and so far, Eric lived up to her expectations: a perfectly mannered, if perfectly intimidated, young gentleman. Though really, she reflected with a sigh, he was barely out of boyhood.

Lady Solivante pulled loose the ties that bound her layered petticoats and freed her voluminous skirts, which fell to the ground to reveal her legs. Slender, elegant, smooth. Perfectly smooth, perfectly metallic. Her young guest made a sound that, although barely audible, she had heard countless times before. She smiled and giggled, raised her eyebrows, and cocked her head to one side. Curling a taloned nail towards him, she beckoned. Even that curving of her finger was slow and awkward, like moving through the deep snow of winter. She ought to be enjoying this encounter because it could well be her last, but just as her flesh was being transformed into a cold and lifeless thing, so were her mind and soul.

Enjoyment, pleasure, comfort—these things were all but lost to her.

The man-boy, Eric, looked about to speak, but instead, his mouth opened and closed uselessly. He looked at his glass and Lady Solivante gestured towards a side table. He placed his Champagne upon it and, after an encouraging nod from her, stepped forwards, his keenness obvious despite his nervousness and inexperience.

She took his hands into her own to guide him to her corset laces and when the cold, hard surface of her hands touched the warmth and softness of her guest, Lady Solivante closed her eyes for a brief moment to savour the rich texture of his skin—yielding, plump, textured. The heat of his skin ...

'Madame?' His voice was shaking, and she opened her eyes again, wondering if she was holding him too tightly. Every day it was harder to tell, harder to feel; she was in danger of losing sensation completely.

'Go ahead, dear one.' Being a gentlewoman and, even now, at this late stage of her infection, still considering herself a Priestess, Lady Solivante took care to be gracious to her visitors. Especially ones who were paying as highly as this specimen. Did that matter any longer, she wondered? Their money and their sponsorship were worthless to her; no matter how wisely her investors acted on her behalf, all of the research she paid for had come to naught. No amount of coin or treasure could help her now, this condition could not be resolved—her dire fate was sealed.

'Once these are free, we shall have the most marvellous and exciting time.' She ran a hand across the top of her breasts and shivered at the touch, the firmness, the smoothness of the metal took the place of her once supple, once soft skin.

After a few moments of fumbling, the corset was discarded, revealing Lady Solivante in all her shining glory. Glimmering with pinpricks of light from the candles, her metal-rich veins pulsating beneath the metal, which once was skin but now shone with sparkling reflections. She was, she well knew, quite breath-taking to behold. In another world, far too long ago, she had been revered as the highest of the Priestesses, but now she was relegated to the status of high-class prostitute. How she had fallen, in her disease.

'Touch me.' Lady Solivante whispered, guiding his hands, and making him claw at her breasts. She pulled at his clothing, her sharp fingers ripping easily through the cotton ruffles of his shirt and so that she could carefully caressing his skin. 'So soft.' She leaned in, to smell his odour, and regretted the long-ago loss of her own natural scent.

'Are you always this cold?' he asked, finding confidence in his excitement.

'Eric, I am eternally cold.'

Lady Solivante let him paw at her, his moist lips roving over her flesh, and she regretted that those sensations of touch and warmth were no longer hers to feel. Only his warmth lent itself to her, seeping into her gradually. So slowly he would not notice it. At least, not yet.

'It won't be enough.' she regretted. It would never be enough.

And perhaps it was time for her to stop trying to make it be enough. The touch of his flesh upon her own was lost to her, yet still she yearned for it, encouraged it, but it did them, her mortal lovers, no good. Her form leeched away their life-force and the urge to take more, more, and more, consumed her every moment.

Her body was almost completely taken over by the living metal spores of the bloody metal infection. She'd acquired it from the forge, where she had wielded powerful tools and built great sculptures, buildings, bridges, machinery, engines, and workings of gold, copper, steel, iron, brass, bronze, silver, titanium, palladium, gelstanium, and irizinium. Ah! Sweet irizinium: that living, breathing, flexible metal of her long-ago home. It was wretched to her now—that vile, immoral, adorable, dangerous substance. What once had been her sole reason for living— oh, the thrill it had given her to be Priestess of that magnificent palace, where engineers held the highest of ranks—was now her downfall and would soon be her death.

The young man moaned, and she stirred into action, caressing him, returning his touches and clasping him to her as they kissed, smothering one another with fiery passion. She urged him on and the living spores of irizinium that infected her, that had caused her limbs to stiffen as metal gradually replaced muscle, bone, sinew, and blood, parted to permit his entry. An instinctive part of her wanted to close up, to push him away and not allow this abomination to happen. If she drank the rich, precious blood hat her body craved, it would leave the man sickly for weeks, perhaps even pass the irizinium infection onto him—it had happened before and killed her guest instantly. They were warned of the risks, these women and men who came to satisfy their dark, lustful urges for the odd, the strange, and unusual. Did that make it right?

No, Lady Solivante thought, that did not make it right, and with this thought her decision was made.

She would not feed off the living energy of this warm-blooded, warm-hearted young man who was paying to experience the wonder of the living metal woman. She would let the irizinium spores consume her completely—they had already claimed her legs, chest, and arms; even her hair and her eyes were being slowly overcome. She feared for the lives of her guests if she insisted on keeping the infection at bay.

Let it have me now, she thought, I have had enough. Let it finish.

Two hundred and seventy years of life the infection had given her, two hundred more than she had any right to claim. She had roamed the galaxies and hunted for a countermeasure but managed only to slow the rate of infection with these infusions her supplicants offered.

'I shall not feed on you.' she said, as he pounded at her in a fevered and frantic rhythm. She wrapped tightly around him, gripping and crying out against the impulse to seize him in a desperate, bloody embrace, fighting the urge to sink her nails into his skin, tear it open, and drink his iron-rich blood in great long draughts.

'I shall not.'

Grunting and panting and coming to his sweet climax, he said nothing, focused only on this moment of rapture, and with every remaining fibre of her natural body she fought that urge to taste the iron of his luscious, warm vital fluid.

'Let it take me.' Lady Solivante cried out. 'Let it end.'

But still she found the taste of his blood in her mouth and the infectious spores of her once-beloved metal, so easy to shape and pleasing to mould, had won out over her humanity again. It was a dual-edged bitter thing, this disease that took over her body and simultaneously made her crave, as strongly as any addiction, the one thing that ameliorated its effects upon her.

The young man, now spent, withdrew himself from her and reeled as he tried to stand, dizzy and light-headed with blood loss, his climax, and the loss of his energy.

With copper tears oozing from her eyes, Lady Solivante reached to her bedside stand and chimed a bell to summon her aides.

Martin and Monrose entered the room and led the bleeding, satisfied, and dizzy young man out of the room and away from their mistress.

Faithful. They would see him home and she knew instinctively that he would not suffer any lasting illness from having his blood taken; she had tasted him and knew he would survive and recover. The iron of his blood raced through every fibre of her mortal body, making her warm for a time, yet in the end only serving to feed the living metal.

Lady Solivante rose from her bed, covered with lace, velvet, satin, fur, and feathers, pristine and freshly laundered or replaced as necessary by her aids. She moved away from the luxurious textures that she could no longer feel, and picked up her looking glass, gazing at her image.

She drew a finger across her neckline, following the curving line of metal where it had crept up to meet her own skin, beneath her chin. The Priestess in her sensed she did not have long.

After sweet young Eric, there had been no others. She dined no longer on the iron of blood to keep the monster of her living metal disease at bay. What would she become in the days and weeks and years to follow? A wild beast craving the tender succulence of mortality? No, she shook her head with melancholic resolve, and molten beads of metal fell from her eyes. She would not be the cause of any more deaths, would not risk any more of those encounters.

Even as she watched, over the course of the year, the bronzing of her skin increased and crept inexorably across her face. She could feel it rippling over the once-warm skin of her cheeks, leaving a cold hard metal in its place. As the infection reached her brow and scalp, so too it wormed inside her head and in her final movement, she dropped the mirror and rose. And became still. And silent.

Trapped inside the metal encasement of her diseased body, no longer possessing the will or power to move—able only to think.

A beautiful structure: a refined sculpture in the shape of an elegant woman, seemingly carved in a bronze-coloured metal, with glittering copper-red eyes and hair of silver and iron with flashes of gold. Standing tall and proud in a pose of strength and grace, one hand outstretched, as if to greet a friend.

Encased in a prison of glass and iron, exhibited in museums across planets and time, with a single slice of information engraved into a gold plate for the visitors who would look upon her and stare in wonder.

LADY AROVASTA SOLIVANTE

High Priestess of the Metalwork Palace
Engineer 1st Class,
Master Craftsman of the Seven Guilds
The Irizinium Priestess—
Graceful to the End of Her Days

THE TALE OF MARY DEVLIN
Geraldine Lambert

AUTUMN 1977

Mary Devlin sits at the wooden table in her office with a mug of Nescafe, two empty milk cartons and four opened British Rail sugar sachets scattered around her. The Ladies' Conveniences Office is small but neatly organised. On the right, next to the old wooden broom, big cylindrical boxes of Vim cluster together within their bulky outer containers. A large industrial radiator pumps out heat, whilst a selection of dried-up cleaning cloths, shrivelled into intricate outlines, lay on top. Their jagged shapes look like distorted eyes, noses, and mouths on stain-infested faces. Beside them are stacked containers of soap and boxes of toilet tissue; some is the industrial tracing paper-type, and some is the more expensive, softer variety, which Mary and many of the women think is a luxurious necessity. They tower in a random pile next to the bleach, sawdust, and metal cleaning buckets. She changes the toilet-rolls around in the cubicles, to confuse the ladies as they select their favourite loo; seeing the women dart from one toilet to another in search of a more comfortable touch is her little bit of fun.

Mary's office is surrounded by large, dated, mottled glass windowpanes. They make it impossible to look into her small claustrophobic space, but she can see abstract colours and disjointed movement as female figures pass by. A large wooden door, with its Bakelite handle and dangling keys, stands guarding her privacy when she doesn't feel sociable. However, on good-mood-days the door stands open so that Mary can chat to the women, as they pass in and out of the outer main area.

MARY

Mary has worked in the ladies' toilets at Cluttersea mainline station for more than 37 years. She began working as an assistant in the station's paper shop when she left school at 15 and applied for the job of cleaner and caretaker of the ladies' public conveniences several years later. She likes the autonomy of having no real boss to manage her and is proud of being part of the team within the British Rail community. The other workers respect Mary and consider her presence to be a big part of the large, busy station's infrastructure.

Mary is a woman in her early fifties, who doesn't seem to 'need much, want much or take much' from life, just like her gypsy forebears from Ireland and East Yorkshire. She wears a pale blue overall to work, which pulls and stretches over her thick-set figure and makes her look more bulky than she really is. Generally, Mary appears to be strong and motherly, and when she smiles her face and eyes light up. However, when crossed, she knows how to stand up for herself, and can appear quite defensive at times. Jeannie from the station café is her best friend and the pair enjoy socializing at the Railway Union Workers' Club during their weekends off. Together, they flirt and flatter the male workers, who often lecture the women about those in charge and the political powers that be, as if they didn't already know, but the women just listen, smile sweetly, and then ask antagonising questions for fun.

Mary finds social politics interesting and knows that many women would hate to clean toilets for a living; the mess, the smell, and the other stuff is sometimes quite offensive. She takes great pride in her traditionally secretive female workplace and takes her responsibilities seriously enough, if done in her own time and on her own terms. But there is also a strange, covert side to Mary's character: when not cleaning, she sits in her office at the back of the cubicles like a spectral women possessed. She stares unseen, like a vixen ready to greet or pounce, watching as women from all walks of life come and go, seeking to help or hinder, as the case may be.

THE USUAL VISITORS

The ladies' loos are discreetly situated in the station and the original Victorian red bricks are internally painted a calming, pale, cobalt blue. Many of the regular visitors like to greet Mary with a nice "Hello" or "Good morning" and share a few coarse or cheerful words about the weather, depending on the season. Time is easy in the ladies' loos, and this agrees with Mary because she can read her tarot cards and books while the hours last forever and the minutes sleepily pass by. However, the silence is broken when the regular ladies pop in and out during the morning rush hour, or later at the end of the day. The working cleaners are usually the first of the day to pop in to relieve themselves, at around 6.30 in the morning. They like Mary because they're all doing manual yet important jobs and as such, they are their own little club. Then there are the shop girls, who trot in smelling of perfume at 8am, their stilettos tapping on the ceramic tiled floor. If they have time, they check their make-up and hair in the shiny mirrors before walking to work in the city's busy shopping centre. Next are the contrastingly dressed art students, clad in their Dr. Martens and punky zip boiler suits, with A1-sized portfolios that are far too large to carry and scrape across the floor. Later, the courtly professional ladies enter, wearing sophisticated tweed skirts and fashionable twinsets. They come to fasten their hair slides, check their hosiery, and apply face powder to disguise their red noses on cold winter mornings.

Later in the afternoon, the surly little youngsters come to pay a visit on their way home from school. They arrive in clusters, wearing short grey skirts and slipping socks, smelling of the 1970s with Charlie and patchouli oil wafting from underneath their gabardine raincoats. They often leave sticky finger marks on the door locks and Mary puts that down to all the toffees and Spangles they stuff in their mouths. The schoolgirls are a bit afraid of the lady who works in the loos and, behind closed doors, they insult one another with the threat of having to be a loo cleaner if no one marries them.

Sometimes, later in the evening there are the 'Nighters', who come in threes and tart themselves up in the mirrors above the sinks, taking ages reapplying their blushers and mascaras. Mary knows they are good-time girls, who operate from Ceasar's disco on the seafront, but she knows they have to make a living. 'If they don't bother me, then I won't bother them' is her motto. Sometimes she reads the Tarot cards for them and tells the girls whether it will be a good night or whether a 'new man' will come on the scene. They see Mary as a maternal figure, and they always smile when she flatters them and promises to keep their hushed-up secrets.

The city is, however, a place where all sorts of people scratch and jostle to earn a living, add value to life, or just to survive. There are the 'wild forgotten souls', as Mary calls them; the undesirables: unwashed, ill-favoured, and wretched, their spirits are lost in the urban sprawl. Some of the feral women are alcoholics, with their saddened cheeks and limp hair, and the homeless come to wash with luxurious free hot water that wipes away the tell-tale city grime. Then there are the mentally ill, who sit begging for change, or loiter around the platform alleys picking up paper and coins from the callous concrete floor. Mary looks out for them, the forgotten women, and gives them yellow-sticker sandwiches or damaged bars of chocolate from the news shop. Their grimy black fingernails and hollow expressions read, 'I am alone. I survive. Don't bother me', but Mary starts brief conversations, giving a touch of much-needed contact and dignity. One homeless woman, who is often harassed by men, sits outside the station shouting abuse at empty-faced passers-by. She protests and swears about the "fucking government" and the so-called "emergency fund." She is often brought a coffee by Mary and Jeannie, the pair of them look out for her in a distant manner, which is not too close to get involved, but close enough to shed a light.
'

BLITZ THE PLACE' WEDNESDAY

So, all these women use the toilets throughout the day, and it is Mary's job to clean, scrub, and freshen the sinks, taps, toilets, floor, and sometimes the wall, to a sanitary condition. She scrubs away the unsightly marks that no one wants to see in the toilets and basins. She also dusts and swipes the windows and disinfects any remnants of human waste: the odd used condom, pregnancy test kit, syringe, wet tissue strewn across the floor, graffiti, chewing gum, tampons (both soiled and clean) and much, much worse. Sometimes, she serves as a lost-property centre, collecting books and papers left on the floor, handbags on the doorknobs, and even a suitcase once. She asked the security manager to check that out, as she felt uncomfortable regarding what might be waiting inside.

    On one drizzly November morning when the cold began to bite, Mary picked up the cloths lying on the radiator to begin her 'Blitz the Place Wednesday'. This took place every single Wednesday throughout the year. It was a thorough deep clean that Mary had devised to keep things looking more than reasonable. She did not just attack the toilet bowls and sinks and taps like the other days—oh no—this cleaning 'blitz' was a 'top-to-toe' treatment, waging war on the places no one usually noticed. The under bowls, the copper pipes, the areas of flooring where tiny fragments lay hidden, the pull handles, mirror screws, enamelled crevices ... All were tugged, rubbed, and polished with bleaches, grit powders, creams, and fresheners.

> "Rub a dub dub, Rub a dub dub,
> Scour the old scud, Scour the old scud,
> Get out a bowl, to clean up the old,
> Rub a dub dub, Rub a dub dub..."

As she frantically rubbed, scoured, scrubbed, wiped, and sterilized for hours at a time, she liked to chant a little rhyme to feed her energy whilst she absolutely hammered the place. Clammy and exhausted when the cleaning session was finished, she stood back to gaze upon her handiwork. The room was transformed into a gleaming crystal palace scented in pine, bleach, and lemon, and the sun poured in pure streams of light upon the brightly glistening white surfaces. The tap handles, levers, and mirrors sparkled unblemished, whilst the floor shone with a dancing vibrancy. Despite her sore and aching limbs, as she stood upright to admire all her hard work she was filled with an energising sense of dignity and great satisfaction. She knew this was something she was really good at, something people noticed, and it filled her with a great sense of pride.

THE UNFAMILIAR PAIR

Later, for a small treat after all her hard work, Mary enjoyed a short break pulling the cards with Jeannie from the café. The start of the afternoon had been fairly quiet, with just an occasional user entering the loo, but then two young women Mary didn't recognize noisily entered the room. One had a softer face than the other, who looked handsome but with harder features. Both women looked quite intriguing, and Mary smiled at the younger of the two, who responded with a short nod. Sat in her office, Mary pretended to read her book, 'Sympathetic Magic and the Law of Contagion', while secretly observing the pair. Their swanky clothing and stylish haircuts amused Mary, as she tried to overhear their conversations on when the ship was due in and where the punters should be greeted. Then they began to whisper and discuss how much they should expect, and what they could accept for this, that, and the other.

    The women continued to comment on their business deals amid their general chit-chat, and Mary had no doubt that they were about to greet the crew of an American ship that was due in port after months at sea. She learnt through their conversation that their names were Paulette and Shareen, and she gleaned from their sentences that they lived somewhere north of Watford. Mary enjoyed eavesdropping while the women continued to whisper about having to get through Christmas and needing to get the holiday cash in. She learnt a lot, in general, from customer chit-chat: where people lived, and who they knew and what they did for a living. Their talk would paint bright images in Marys' mind of glamorous people living lives of travel and adventure and dramatic love affairs.

So, Paulette and Shareen stood there, taking their time sorting through items in their carry bags, while stripping off to redress themselves in their new frippery, as Mary watched their gradual transformation. She noticed how obsessed and determined they were in creating appearances as arousing and thrilling as possible. There were seamed stockings, black chokers, velvet miniskirts, waist cinchers, bras stuffed with socks, low-cut V-neck black tops, serpent jewellery, and the alluring scent of Musk, which overpowered the familiar whiff of Vim and bleach. Then there was the rest of it … The women went on to blend different lotions, potions, powders, and puffs all over their faces and décolletés. Large fat pencils were smudged and blended, penis-shaped lipsticks slipped hues of rose and crimson upon their lips, and liquid fake tans caressed their shimmering skin in shades of orange.

Mary surveyed this pantomime of glamourie and transformation from young, fresh-faced lassies into exhilarating and extraordinary sex magnets. She was bemused at how some women went about their ways: the ones endowed with big boobs, fat bottoms, general good looks, and glittering smiles. How they spoke, where they went, where they lived, their families and friends ... she constantly compared their very different lives to her own.

But then, after a short silence Mary overheard Paulette and Shareen playing a word game, while she continued to pretend to read her magical book. She wasn't sure at first why they were just saying random words, followed by lots of mirth and laughter afterwards. They kept exchanging looks between their chuckles, and Mary saw them peering from mirror to her and back again. As she sat there, trying to put two and two together, with a pain in her chest and much humiliation she slowly realized that they were describing her own dowdy appearance.

Their sense of descriptive order was random; her meaty feet, bristled chin, dingy overall, clumpy legs, pongy quim ... The silly name calling carried on, whilst Shareen and Paulette competed with one another for the next response. However, it was the term "pug butt" that made them both scream with laughter, as both women knew its hidden slang meaning. While they continued to take the piss out of the dreary, middle-aged stranger, Mary pretended not to listen and sat there—sullied and crestfallen.

FALL AND REVENGE

It was the loss of face within her own surroundings that made Mary's pride give way and fall. Her self-respect and ego descended into dismal humiliation that was especially acute following, as it did, the high from all her hard cleaning that morning. Mary often laughed at herself with people she knew, but on this occasion, as her hurt and irritation grew, she began to feel a hot anger rise and burn in response to the women's laughter. So, while the pair continued to preen themselves in the mirror, taking such pride in their self-satisfied charisma, Mary determined to take her revenge. Placing her book on the table, she decided to experiment with her favourite magical process:

'... for when two objects (either animate or inanimate) come into contact with each other, there is a potentially permanent exchange of properties between them.' Hastily picking up one of the cotton cloths and disturbing the gaze of both girls in the process, she unexpectedly began to vigorously scrub the mirror as they both gawked into it. Mouths opened in shock and surprise, and they both cried, "What the fuck ...?" but Mary continued to swipe over the glassy surface, stealing their reflections, and softly chanting:

"Rub a dub dub, Rub a dub dub,
Your face I will scrub,

your face I will scrub,
From every direction,
I'll catch your reflection,
Rub a dub, Rub a dub dub ..."

As Mary concentrated on swiping and absorbing the imprint of Paulette and Shareen's reflected image, she couldn't help but notice the mess all over the recently cleaned sinks, for they were now covered in smears and spills of sludge and gloop. Dots of cheap pink, black, and grey pigment had sprayed onto the walls, and stray bronzing lotion looked like chewed orange toffee and diarrhoea splotched around the taps and plugs. Mary was angry—very angry—but the rising level of her fury did not affect her concentration. On the contrary, it fed her potent determination, as she continued to mutter and swipe the smeared, glassy surface, fuelling the intention of her spell.

Paulette and Shareen hurriedly left the ladies' WC with their carry bags and Trotter heels; the tassels and belts on their black jackets trailing behind them. Their posture betrayed their fallen guise, for they had been shaken by Mary's sudden erratic behaviour and strange ramblings into thin air.

SWEET PRIDE, RETURNED

So, once the two girls had gone and when all was nice and quiet again, Mary daintily stretched out the dirty cleaning cloths that had collected the girls' reflections and delicately placed them over the large radiator in her office. The textured fabric hissed as Mary placed the cloths across the burning metal spires, bending and distorting with shrinkage, while popping with a blistering tension. Mary paid particular scrutiny to the progress of the images that appeared as gnarled markings, twisted and evolved beyond recognition. And as her thoughts of Intent and Will deepened, she trusted that those formerly striking faces would develop and emerge as those hideously malformed masks of cloth. While focussing, she quietly muttered, "I bet you both look as rough as a bear's arse now!" Then, as she closed her eyes to concentrate, her inner mind took her to a street by the harbour, where the big ships come in ...

Amidst the hordes of sailors in their uniforms, Mary sees some spritely, sparky women and ... but wait, there is Paulette and Shareen. The pair look disgruntled and dishevelled, their faces soiled and fractured with smudged shadows and textured popping marks of purple, grey, and green. Their once-sassy hair has turned into dull clumps of flat, frayed-looking string, and their hands and fingers are rough and bleeding with scratched, torn skin, as though they had been scrubbed with Brillo pads and scouring powder. With swollen arms and bloated features, Paulette and

Shareen appear blurred and skittish as they hysterically point, while shouting and squealing at one another. Their fissured lips are cracked like shattered glass, and their bobbing, ulcerated cheeks flicker and flare with a mucus discharge. As they try to embrace the sailors, they are both quickly turned away—spurned—as their selected clients grimace with confusion and call out cries of disgust.

When Mary had finished her reverie, she thought light-heartedly that they wouldn't be pulling the cocks tonight. She chuckled to herself whilst drying her hands and checked her watch before leaving for the day.

With her outmoded beige coat and tatty scarf in hand, Mary hummed a familiar tune as she left the station building. It hadn't been an ordinary day after all, she thought to herself.

She smiled and felt quite uplifted, for she had taken great Pride in her handiwork.

THE AFTERMATH

Pride has a strange effect on us all. We feel the comforting raise in our self-admiration, but we are often blind to its effect in our everyday life. And Mary, sadly, was no exception. She continued to work at the railway conveniences for another 12 months or so and continued to enjoy the buzz and gratification that her hard work brought her. However, this was to such an extent, that she increased her 'Blitz The Place' endeavour to every other day, not just Wednesdays.

Regretfully, the awareness of the dangers and hazards found in cleaning chemicals was not readily available during the 1970s. The spitting fumes from all the ammonia, caustic soda, phosphates, and acids found within the disinfectants, bleaches, and polishers that she used daily had a bad effect on her aging body. The high levels of exposure began to accumulate and place a toxic burden upon Mary's lungs and endocrine system.

At first, Mary refused to acknowledge what was happening to her overall energy and general health, but slowly and surely her hair began to dry out and fall, and her cough began to scratch and burn. When she noticed the brittle clumps in her hairbrush, she knew that it was time to leave her much-loved workplace. On her final day she received an award for 'The Best Cleaner Southwest Railways 1979'. She said farewell to her colleagues and began her much anticipated retirement.

Mary now sits every day in her small garden, which is meticulously arranged with wild colourful flowers and silver-leafed shrubs that sparkle with the sun and glint in the moonlight. There is no stone left unturned. As she sits at her garden table, with her books, cards, and coffee, she knows that all is well, for in her garden the rain does her washing whilst the wind dries it and the sun nurtures all to perfection. Mary's Pride has found a peaceful serenity within the allure and beauty of Nature.

SLOTH

SLOTH
Diane Narraway

Manyana is my battle cry.
As the dust begins to pile,
I'll do it later;
I'll do it in a while.

The diet, well, that can wait,
The fat ain't going nowhere.
And perhaps tomorrow
I'll even brush my hair.

Yeah, I could get up off the couch,
But I don't really see the need.
I have the quilt, TV remote,
And the takeaway guy has a key.

And I'm quite happy here,
And my ever-increasing pile
Of empty boxes and other trash
Brings me comfort, and a smile.

Besides, some of it doubles
As a very handy latrine.
Well, waste not want not,
And it's upcycling, I believe.

Well, this has been an effort,

I could do with a nap.
I'll finish it tomorrow …

NOT GUILTY
Marisha Kiddle

I woke up in a pool of sweat, my body was shivering, and my head was hurting—Flu!

I rang up work and booked my sick time off,

"About a week should do it," I told Dawn.

"No probs, Margo will hold the fort while you're away." Dawn replied.

Margo was a temp: whenever one of us was ill, on holiday, or we had too much on, she stepped in and helped us out. We could have done with her working in the office full-time, but the boss, Brian, wouldn't pay out for another full-time member.

I took some tablets and snuggled into my duvet, hoping that relief would come quickly to my aching body.

I awoke six hours later to my husband, Colin, coming home from work. Upon finding me ill, he took care of dinner for us and our two kids, Damon aged eight and Brianna aged fifteen. They all helped with the things I needed, such as tissues, the remote for my TV, and the odd cup of tea. I quite liked the attention, and enjoyed being waited on hand and foot while I was curled up in my duvet.

A few days later I started to feel better, but I had got used to being fussed over. Dawn had messaged, to ask if I had any idea when I would be returning to work because we had received a large order. It needed sorting out, and so, I was needed back in the office as soon as possible. Colin was under pressure too, working all day then coming home and having to do all the cooking and cleaning.

After I had been in bed for about a week, my flu had passed, and I knew I should be getting back to my job, my kids, and my husband, but it was so nice not having to do anything or go anywhere. I opened up Google and started searching for illnesses that couldn't be easily identified. I found one, researched everything I could about it, and then, rang my doctor's surgery and requested a sick note for work.

That evening, when Colin got home from work, I explained to him that I had spoken to our doctor, and he had advised me to get plenty of rest; the flu had knocked my immune system for six and it could take me months to recover fully. He looked tired, but I didn't care—I had done everything for years. Ok ... not totally alone, like Colin was now, he had always helped me around the house. But hey, it was OK ... I was ill, right?

Over the coming weeks I told friends and family that there were some things that I couldn't do, I was always just too tired and too weak. In truth, I felt great! The kids stopped running around after me as much as they had at the beginning, but that was OK. I could still get them to do some stuff for me, even if they did complain about it. Colin was forever patient and continued doing all the chores that needed to be done; he became quite adept at doing the washing, after I'd moaned at him for not splitting the whites and colours.

Dawn, however, was becoming increasingly frustrated. Things needed doing at work and I wasn't there to do them. Margo had been working non-stop, but she had work she needed to do. She wasn't meant to be there permanently, and she wasn't trained to do the work that I did.

Did I feel guilty? Nope, not one bit.

Weeks turned to months ... When no one was in the house, I would dance around the front room, read books, and play games on my phone. But as soon as they came home, I would lay in my bed and pretend not have enough energy to do even the simplest of tasks. Dawn had not spoken to me for ages, and we used to be quite close. Friends who would normally have invited me to dinner, or to parties, stopped asking. My husband had started to lose weight and became tired and withdrawn; I can't remember the last time I saw him smile.

Did it bother me? Nope, I still didn't care.

A year later, so much has changed. Margo was given my job, my wages were reduced to statutory sick pay, and I have no friends left. None of them text or phone me anymore. The worst thing was my husband leaving and taking the kids with him. He said that obviously I wouldn't be able to cope with looking after them, and that he had to leave because he couldn't cope on his own anymore. Yep, you read that right. He had met someone else and was planning to set up home with her.

So, here I am, 2 years on, and still lazily wallowing, with not a care in the world about anyone except myself. I hope Colin is happy with Dawn, they are well suited.

And me, well I've started collecting plush sloths—they are so cute!

BELPHEGOR
Bekki Milner

The screams of the tortured souls thrown into the pit of snakes usually brought great joy to Belphegor. This morning, though, his lips didn't even form a smile as he peered out the window, which was a rough stone opening, hewn in his cavernous house overlooking the snake-pit.

Fresh souls had arrived just last night, and it was usually so invigorating watching them dance around the writhing floor, great mouths snapping at their heels, lush green bodies winding around limbs to squeeze eternally. Today, he barely managed a sneer.

Maybe he was hungry. What was it Beelzebub had called it ... hangry? That was it. Belphegor was surely hangry.

In the kitchen he prepared his favourite breakfast: devilled eggs and hot black coffee. The food was good, but not good enough to break his mood. Even the cold nose of his pet goat, Inertia, raised nothing but a scowl, and she scurried back to her basket in a hurry, sensing Belphegor's mood.

Letting his coffee cup drop back to the table with a quiet thud, Belphegor sighed. As he gazed around the room, his eyes found his to-do list carved upon the wall. He was usually well-prepared and laid out his to-do list the night before.

At the top, there was a meeting with the Seven at 9am. This was followed by snake management, and checking in on Victor Hugo and his writing. His afternoon was free, a time when Belphegor would usually enjoy some of his favourite pastimes: visiting his human wife in Italy or tinkering with one of the many machines that littered his grand cavern in Pandemonium.

But today Belphegor didn't want to do any of that. He didn't want to sit around the table with the rest of the Seven, or introduce new snakes to the pit, or visit his beautiful Onesta. She had been spending a lot of money of late, he realised, and he wasn't sure he was really in for the long haul with this marriage. It was all Satan's fault; he was the one who had sent him to find out if such a thing as married happiness existed on earth. The debt that was slowly growing had already convinced him otherwise.

Belphegor sighed. Looking at the clock, an intricate timepiece he had made himself, he had twenty minutes before Asmodeus would arrive at his door to walk to the meeting together, as he always did. The idea of listening to him drone on about the men and women he'd screwed the night before made his heart sink even more.

He rested his head upon the table, pushing his plate aside and groaning at the sheer thought of having to sit in another meeting with the other Seven Kings of Hell. He'd never wanted to be part of this anyway; the father had only cast him out for being idle in choosing a side when Lucifer declared war against Heaven. Now he had no choice but to take part in their ridiculous meetings around the stone table, while the lower demons gossiped about him only being there because he was good with machines, and Lucifer needed that.

Belphegor was roused from his thoughts by a knock on the cavern door. Screwing his eyes closed, he clenched his teeth and hoped Asmodeus would leave if he ignored him long enough. However, the Lord of Lust was not so easily deterred by a closed door and had performed this morning ritual so often he just let himself in to Belphegor's home, as if he lived there.

'Good morning, Belphegor. I hope you are ready for the meeting. It's a gloriously dark day out, the realms of hell are glowing with the pain of tortured sinners. You won't need a jacket, it's quite mild.' Asmodeus announced, his claws clicking on the stone floor.

Belphegor opened one lazy eye that rolled over Asmodeus from head to toe. The triple-headed King of Hell filled the doorway with his fierce physique; when he wasn't wooing mortals to their certain death, he was in the gym.

He winced as Asmodeus' tail flicked too close to one of his creations, the pulleys and wheels whining in protest before it tumbled to the floor with a crash. Belphegor groaned and buried his head in his hands again, as Asmodeus' first head, the bull, took in the damage. The ram bleated in protest at their clumsiness and his middle head, that of a man, winced awkwardly.

'Asmodeus, please, be careful. That was six weeks' worth of work you just destroyed.' He pushed himself up off the table to retrieve the wreckage from the floor. He tossed it back on the sideboard, shaking his head.

'I don't think I'm coming today; you go on without me.' Belphegor sank into his comfy chair, a gust of air creaking from the leather beneath his weight.

Asmodeus was visibly taken back. None of the Kings of Hell had ever been absent from a meeting, and he wasn't quite sure how to react. His mouths opened and closed simultaneously, the bull and the ram emitting soft grunts of confusion, while the centre head fixed Belphegor with a shocked stare.

'What do you mean, "not going"? What will I say to the others? Lucifer will have your head, you know.' The ram nodded in agreement and the bull snorted, shaking its ears.

'I don't feel like it today.' Belphegor shrugged, leaning further back in the chair, with no intention of going anywhere, whether it was mild out or not. He pressed his fingers together, elbows on the arm of the chair, and watched Asmodeus confer with his other heads in low whispers. The ram was visibly distressed.

Asmodeus turned sharply to the door as if to leave through it, only to disappear in a puff of smoke before he'd even opened it. The smell of sulphur lingered in the yellow cloud and Belphegor rolled his eyes. No doubt Asmodeus had gone to fetch back-up. He wondered which of the other five Lords he'd get to come and help. He didn't have to wait long.

There was a great buzzing outside the door and hushed, concerned whispers made Belphegor's ears twitch; he sighed, waiting for them to settle their plan. The door creaked open slowly.

The flies came first: great swathes of them in murmuration swirled around his living room, landing wherever they pleased. Belphegor swatted them away from his face, watching Beelzebub follow them in. Behind them, Asmodeus leant on the doorway like a demonic heartthrob on a cheap romance book cover.

'Belphegor! What's up with you?' Beelzebub buzzed through sharp teeth and plump, purple lips. Though short in stature, his rams' horns shone black as night, and his skin was a healthy shade of red. His wings, taller than he stood, folded neatly against his back.

'Asmodeus here tells me you're not coming to the meeting. Is that right?' Beelzebub raised a neatly plucked eyebrow. In that moment, with his thin, trimmed moustache, he looked every bit a Sailor Jerry devil. Belphegor suppressed a chuckle.

'Asmodeus is right. I'm not going. I don't feel like it.' Belphegor sank back against the seat again and folded his arms over his chest, to emphasise his point.

'Ah, come on; it's not that bad. It'll be over in no time.' Beelzebub grinned, punching Belphegor's arm gently in jest. 'You know the drill. Lucifer will reel off the day's soul count, Satan will have his usual rant, Leviathan will make his usual speech about getting less attention than the rest of us, Mammon will ask for another rise, and I,' he puffed out his chest, 'I will eat all the donuts.' He grinned, a fly crawling over his nose and into his hairline.

'And I will stay right here.' Belphegor waited to see what Beelzebub would come up with next.

'Belphegor ... Bels ... listen. We both know that if you're a no-show, Lucifer will come and get you himself.' Asmodeus said from the door, the ram and the bull nodding in agreement.

'Asmodeus is right! He will!' Beelzebub nodded. 'And you know he won't be happy about it.'

Belphegor glanced at the clock. It was four minutes to nine o' clock. He knew that Asmodeus and Beelzebub were right: Lucifer would not be happy. Yet something inside him just dismissed any wrath or ire he could possibly face.

'Very well.' He said, resolutely. Beelzebub's shoulders dropped in relief and Asmodeus breathed a heavy sigh. Belphegor chuckled to himself as he rose from his chair and turned to face them both. 'Let him be unhappy. I'm going back to bed.'

Four jaws dropped in total, the ram bleating in protest, Beelzebub's wings fluttering with angst, his flies buzzing in unison. Belphegor ignored their pleas, turning his back on them and heading for his bedchamber.

'Now what will we do?' Asmodeus was panicking.

'I don't know! We're going to be late ourselves if we don't leave.' Beelzebub flailed his arms, exasperated.

'Baaaa!' the ram chimed in.

'Let's go. Let Lucifer deal with him.'

Asmodeus shrugged. The two left, the scent of sulphur drifting through the cavern. Belphegor slipped into his bed, back beneath the duvet, and closed his eyes. He would sleep the day away and forget about meetings and duties and responsibilities.

Or he would if his feet weren't wet. Something dripped steadily on to the end of the bed. Opening one eye, he peered down to find the scaly sly face of Leviathan peering back at him. Water dripped from his alligator muzzle as it stretched into the kind of grin that showed how much Leviathan was going to enjoy telling him what he had to say.

'You should know ...' he began, sliding the rest of his body on to the bedstead, his tail dropping heavily on to Belphegor's legs. 'Lucifer is on his way.'

Leviathan propped his chin up on a claw, licking his lips in anticipation of what would go down when Lucifer did appear.

'Do you mind? You're wet.' Belphegor pulled his blankets away from Leviathan's dripping alligator form, retreating to the head of his bed. 'How long have you been there anyway?'

'I overheard Asmodeus asking Beelzebub for help,' Leviathan smirked, 'so I slipped in while you were busy dealing with him and his fleas.'

Belphegor tugged the duvet around him and turned his back on the scaly demon, who still dripped water into a puddle on the mattress.

'Don't say I didn't warn you. You had a chance to just be late, instead of not showing up at all.' Leviathan hissed. The dripping stopped, and from the smell of sulphur that was left behind, Belphegor assumed Leviathan had given up and gone. Good, he thought. All he wanted to do was ... nothing. Nothing at all. No demonic duties, no meetings, no discussing the ongoings of Hell—nothing. Finally, snug beneath the duvet, eyes closed, claws and wings tucked away, he was ...

... Floating. He was floating. Belphegor felt his body rise off the bed, felt the duvet snatched away. He opened one eye and saw nothing, the darkness of Lucifer's approach a black cloud that surrounded him.

'Belphegor.' A voice in the dark that dripped honey and sulphur. It always made Belphegor shiver whenever Lucifer used that voice. 'Your presence was lacking at the gathering this morning.'

Belphegor looked around the darkness for the source of the voice, but it came from everywhere within the cloud. He swallowed, not really sure what would happen next. He hadn't really considered it, so determined was he to give up on his duties.

'Yes. Er. Sorry.' Belphegor muttered, unsure what else he could say. The mists cleared a little, a growing, red-tinged white light encircled him as Lucifer appeared from the darkness. Wings aloft, his long, red, perfectly wavy hair shining as it always did, Lucifer's androgynous features looked neither happy nor angry. He was a blank, emotionless canvas. He stopped right before Belphegor, a foot or so away from his face.

'You're guilty, Belphegor. I'm afraid you must face the consequences.' Lucifer's red eyes shone, and Belphegor swore they saw right through to his soul. Or would have if he had one, but that was long gone, he remembered.

'Guilty of what?' Belphegor was a demon, surely he couldn't be guilty in a way that bore any consequence? Were there consequences for demons in hell? This wasn't a rule he was familiar with.

'Guilty of sloth.' Lucifer smirked. 'You have neglected your spiritual duty.' He licked his top lip, as if to savour the moment. 'You must face the punishment.'

'Punishment? But I'm a Lord of Hell!' Belphegor raged against unseen restraints and Lucifer cawed with laughter.

'Oh Belphegor, you work for me! Neglecting your duties is not without punishment!' Lucifer waved a hand and the mists dispersed, revealing the pit of snakes below them.

Great green and gold bodies writhed, and jaws snapped in anticipation of their next meal. The sound that left Belphegor's throat would have made him happy on any overly bright Hell morning, he realised; just as it pleased Lucifer, the Dark Lord, grinning at the sound of another tortured soul as he watched from the window above.

WRATH

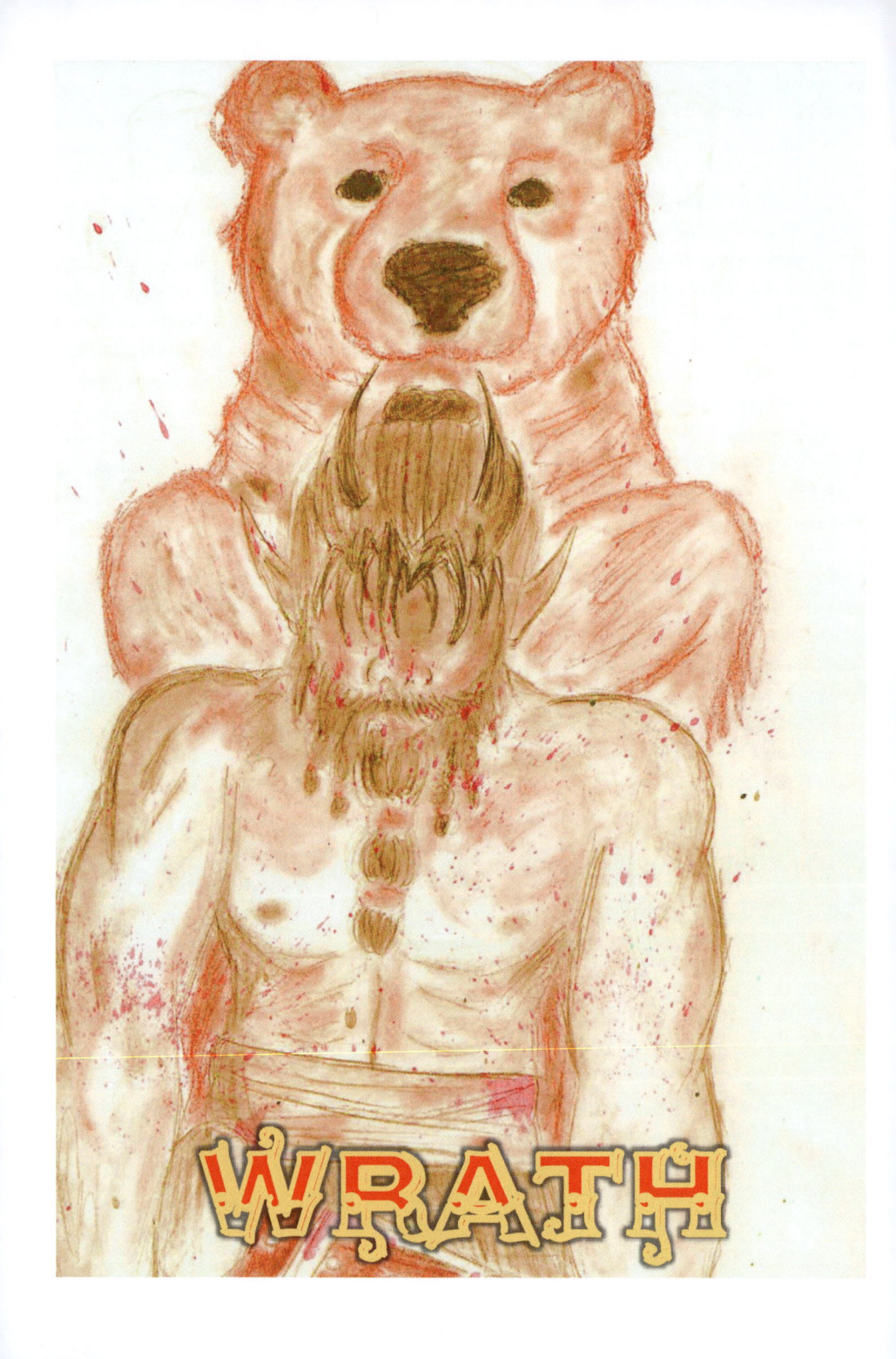

WRATH
Scarlett Paige

You'll see red,
And I will burn
Deep within,
Until you learn.

And there I'll stay,
Trapped in a cage
As that burn
Turns to rage.

While intense fury
Blackens your soul,
I relish the moment
You'll lose control.

The power's then mine,
To torture lovers,
And turn men
Against their brothers.

Success I measure
By the look on the face
Of angels and men,
As they fall from grace.

And to justify your actions,
I'm sure you will try,
But divine retribution
Is a dangerous lie.

I saw your pain,
And you let me in.
Iniquitous wrath,
The deadliest sin.

THE WRATH OF ANN FIELDS
Kate Knight

I wish they would just get on with it. I have told them that I have no remorse and never will. He deserved everything he got. Just light the damn wood and let my life be done, because it is no life without my children. I have no purpose, and no desire to continue to breathe air without them.

These people all stare at me, some with tears of sadness while others chant,

"Murderer. Murderer."

It's obvious who the mothers are amongst the crowd. They pity me and I expect that a fair amount of them would have done the same as I if their children had suffered such as mine did. My beloved daughters; my sweet, sweet angels. They wait for me; I can see them now, in the night sky lit by the torch, as the handler approaches my pyre. A man of faith, I have no doubt, muttering the ramblings of his so-called God in his inebriated state. I believed in him once; I read from the great book and found only nonsense, but I believed, nevertheless. More fool me.

I also believed the man dressed as a messenger of God, when he promised my daughters good teachings and education, drawing them into the woodland for a lesson in the fresh air only to detach their heads from their bodies. He claimed that he had cleansed them from their sins, their souls free to enter the kingdom of heaven. They had no sin. They were the innocents; their only sin in the eyes of that clergyman was the gift of an imagination.

A single mention of the fairy folk that live only in their stories was enough for him to wield his silver knife and hack at their throats. I can only guess that they fought him, as he was covered in not only my girls' blood, but also his own. He returned for his effects, and that was his biggest mistake. He returned thinking that I would thank him for ridding me of my burden of being a lone parent. His ever-lustful thoughts towards me would, in his eyes, be achieved in the hope he may sire new, purer children, replacing my own sinful offspring. Well, he thought wrong, didn't he? He thought wrong. Light the damn fire and let me burn. Release my soul so that I can be with my children forever.

"Any last words? Witch."

"Aye. I have many and you will hear them now before I burn. That God you speak of is here with me now and he hangs his head in shame. My so-called victim murdered my girls, tore their sweet heads from their bodies, and left them in the woods for the wild animals to feast upon. My heart broke open, wide enough to allow a demon to crawl inside my black, witch heart. I tore his exposed manhood from his groin with my bare hands and tossed it into the pigpen. If you want them back, you will have to slice open the belly of my hog and put the chewed-up pieces back together.

While he was writhing in agony, the crows glided down and plucked his eyes from his skull. They flew to the trees with his eyes in their beaks, so he could witness his own sins and see the horror of what was left of his victims. The hounds of hell took his limbs, the meat was required to feed their own young. Why waste good meat, after all? For his sins and my satisfaction, I sliced open his chest and scooped out his heart with my soup ladle. It bled with blood as black as the night. Still, it floats with seasoning and vegetables in the iron pot that hangs over the ashes of last night's fire. The devil will linger in this place and curse all that live here. He will spoil your crops and starve your cattle, and no baby will bless this town again. This place will suffer forever and will only be cleansed when they understand the power behind the wrath of a mother."

What the hell is he doing, dousing me with holy water? Such a foolish endeavour.

"Just get on with it!"

Okay, here goes. This is it. I can already feel the heat. I will look up to the faces of my girls. I can clearly see them now as the sky glows with the growing fire at my feet. They are happy and are reaching for me.

"Not long now my angels. Mother's coming."

I will stay silent; I will stay silent. Deep breaths, get that smoke into my lungs, hopefully it will release me quicker. Jesus, it burns but I will not give these damn people the satisfaction of my cries. I will not. Just breathe ...

At last I am free.

"Come on girls, let's get away from this hell, it's filled with demons."

*

Witness ....

My name is Molly, and I lived in the town of Greysley when Miss Anne Fields was executed. It was believed that she murdered a clergyman, and then took her own children to the woods and beheaded them. That was what we were told, anyhow. The priest denied the accusation that the clergyman was to blame for the girls' murder, as Ann started in her last words, but whispers were rife through the town of the true crime.

Any mother would have done what she did, given the circumstances. She loved those girls and raised them with good manners and wanted only what was best for them. None of us truly believed that she killed them. It was her that put a curse on the town, and those who didn't pack up and leave after she died soon saw the curse at work. The cattle stopped eating, it was as if their mouths wouldn't open, even if we tried to force-feed them. The crops would grow no more than an inch or two from the ground, and not a single woman with child at the time carried to term, the infants all died during the pregnancy, or were still-born.

Dorean Miller fled with her husband the day after Ann died, and gave news of a healthy birth a month later from the next town along. Dorean was Ann's friend, so she knew her well.

We were in the town square when they torched her. She looked up into the sky the entire time. Not once did she scream, not even as her skin melted from her bones. I swear now that it was not only me who saw the faces of those young, murdered girls in the smoke above the pyre. We all said it was like they were waiting to take her soul away.

What was left of the clergyman was buried in the crypt of the church, but a few nights later some people came and took his body away in a blacked-out carriage. I'm not sure why. I was told that his eyes were missing, and that only the head and torso was left. The strange thing is that he also had marks on his throat, like an animal's death bite. Only, no dog around here is big enough to cause a wound that big.

We tried to do what was right, and buried what was left of the girls. Some say two eyes, shrivelled like marbles, were perched on a fallen tree overlooking the bodies, but I'm not sure if there is truth in that. The entire area has all but gone now. The ground took on too much water and turned the whole area into a lake. You can just about see the church spire sticking out of the water. Only two mounds of earth peek out from the waters, and they are covered with sweet green grass: the graves of the two girls. In the spring, flowers cover the mounds, but no one dares to go near because even to this day, the area is said to be guarded by unseen beasts that howl throughout the nights, and cursed by the wrath of Ann Fields.

THE HAND OF WRATH
Scott Irvine

This morning began just like any other morning: I dragged myself out of bed, had a pee, and made myself a cup of tea to ease me into the new day. I watched the news, dominated by the government leadership challenge and massive hikes in energy prices, and have to turn it off before I get too depressed. The next stage of my awakening process is a roll-up in the garden to get my lungs active. I go into the back garden, to catch the late-spring morning sun, and that is when I came across the hand. It was just lying there in the middle of the lawn—a man's left hand, severed cleanly at the wrist. For a moment all I can do is stare at it in disbelief, wondering how it got there, whom it belonged to, and what the hell was I going to do with it. After finishing my roll-up I phoned work, telling them I would be in late because I had a hand to deal with. I phoned the police, who arrived within the hour. After examining it for around fifteen minutes, they deduced that it belonged to a white male of around sixty years of age. A mark on his wedding finger showed that he was married and the ring was missing. I was expecting them to bag it up and take it away with them, but they just told me to bury it in the garden.

'What about fingerprints?' I asked, 'To find out who he was.' The police told me they did not have the resources for things like that anymore, because of government cutbacks, and they had more important things to attend to. It was a case of finders keepers and have a nice day. I was shocked, to say the least. I looked down at the hand to examine it in more detail. There were no marks on it to suggest that it had been dragged there by a wild animal or dropped from the sky by a large bird, or something. The hand, apart from not being attached to a body, looked to be in pristine condition, as if it had only recently been cut off. I couldn't just leave it there and go to work, so I found an old tin big enough to hold the hand, buried it amongst the rose bushes, and said a few words of prayer before leaving for work. I would give it a proper ceremony in the evening, when I got home.

*

I was home earlier than expected, thanks to a big argument with my boss when I got in to work around lunchtime. I was informed that I would have my pay deducted for having the morning off without good reason. What the fuck! Finding a dead hand in your garden is not a good reason? I can't believe I said a dead hand; of course, it was dead, but it only led to my boss not believing my story and accusing me of lying. I told him that if I wanted to lie, I could have made up a better story than that. The argument got heated and I was ordered off the premises and suspended for a week without pay. I was going to wait until my girlfriend Vivienne came over this evening to perform a funeral ritual for the hand, because she was more attuned to the spirit realm and the ways of a witch than me, but I decided I needed to give it some sort of send-off as soon as possible. I dragged my cauldron from the shed, got it stoked up and lit, then called up the Babylonian goddess of death Ereshkigal to receive the hand into her custody in the underworld. I was still angry with the treatment I got at work, and after I had finished the funeral rites, I called on the goddess Ishtar to calm my mind and fill it with love.

*

I had cooked a vegetarian stir-fry for Viv when she came over. She thought my experience with the hand was amusing but was as shocked as I was that the police did not take it away. We searched online for news of anyone losing a hand in Weymouth and the surrounding areas, but to no avail. Viv told me about the 'Hand of Fatima', that Islamists used for protection and to ward off the evil eye, so I assumed the hand I found in the garden was probably a good omen. She was not sure my funeral ritual should have been to Ereshkigal, as she thought other goddesses were more suitable, but as long as the hand had received prayers, Viv saw no reason to give it another ceremony; after all, it was only a hand.

*

The next morning, I had a visit from the police, who wanted to interview me for the murder of my boss. What The Fuck! I was their main suspect after yesterday's altercation with him. He was found strangled in his bed, when his wife came home from her nightshift at the hospital. Lucky for me, Viv had stayed the night and was my alibi. The policemen seemed happy with my statement and left. Viv and me were shocked at the news; my boss, John, was a bit of a dick at times, but didn't deserve to die like that. Viv admonished me for my anger issues, something that she admitted scared her sometimes. I do not consider myself an angry person, but I do like to stand up for myself and speak my mind. When Viv finally left for work, I decided to have a bonfire in the garden and burn some hedge cuttings that had been waiting to be disposed of for a number of weeks. How was I to know my next-door neighbour was about to hang her washing out? The fire was well ablaze when she came out and had a right go at me, stating civil laws and what not. I simply told her my fire was here first, and her washing would have to wait. She called me a few choice words, I responded in kind, and thought nothing more of it.

The following day, the police arrived at my door again; a different pair from yesterday: a male and female. I was implicated in another murder. This time, it was my next-door neighbour who had been strangled, and I had been seen arguing with her, and this time I had no alibi. However, I was not under suspicion, because it had the same modus operandi as the murder of my boss. Forensics had discovered that he had been strangled with a single hand around his throat, which was unusual, and could only have been carried out by someone with super-human strength. I asked if they were both killed by a left hand, but that information could not be revealed. I mentioned the severed hand that I had found in my garden two days earlier, and they laughed at my suggestion that a disembodied hand had committed murder. Even so, I told them I was getting a little concerned and worried that people I knew, and recently argued with, were being murdered soon afterwards. Was the hand cursed? At the very least, something strange was happening around me. The police fingerprinted me before they left, still sniggering at my suggestion of a killer hand on the loose. When they had gone, I phoned Viv, asking her to come over after work and to bring her books on ancient curses with her.

After I had made tea for us both, we went through some of the books Viv had brought over and found a story about the "Hand of Glory", where a hand was cut off of a recently hung criminal, and a wick was added, turning it into a candle that would render anyone it was presented to motionless. After a lot of thought, we decided to dig it up in the morning and hand it into the local mortuary, and if they didn't want it, we would burn it.

    The next morning, after breakfast, I dug the tin box up, only to find it was empty—the hand had disappeared. We were both baffled, but to be honest, I was glad it had gone; I felt that my responsibility for it had gone too, and began to relax a little.

*

    Sunday morning, for me, is all about playing football for the over 30s Weymouth Wizards FC. We are second in the Dorset League Four, and a win today against the top team, Parkstone Removals, would put us top by two points. It was an important game and we had to be at our best to get a result. We started well, going 2-0 up in the first twenty minutes, before they pulled one back on the half-hour mark. Just before half- time, I received the ball in my own penalty box, beat two players and made my way to the half-way line. The opposition kept backing off, expecting me to pass it, as I carried on towards their goal. Their defence just opened up and very quickly, I was in their penalty area, with just the goalkeeper to beat. Before I could shoot, some bastard tripped me up and the ball rolled safely into the grateful arms of the goalkeeper. I was pissed off, but as my team's penalty-taker I just dusted myself off, and prepared to take the penalty, only for the referee to shout 'Play on' and accuse me of diving. I exploded into a rage with the ref, not only for denying me my penalty, but for accusing me of being a cheat too. My ego could not take that, and I had to be dragged away from the cowering referee and made to calm down. I guess I should have been grateful that the referee only booked me, and didn't send me off, for my outrage towards him. I soon calmed down and got on with the game. Anyway, all of that was irrelevant in the end, as we won 3-2 and I scored the winner, with a flying header at the back post. They guy who fouled me apologised afterwards, in the pub. He said that he was as surprised as me that it wasn't a penalty, shook my hand, and bought me a pint. That is what football is all about.

*

That following Tuesday, I got a phone call from my football manager informing me that the referee of Sunday's game was found dead in his bed. He had been strangled. What the fuck was going on?

That evening, Vivienne came round with her smudge stick, crystals, and incense, to cleanse and purify my flat, to rid me of any evil attachments that were lingering in the shadows.

Me: 'Do you think it will work?'

Viv: 'I don't know. I hope so, but I have never heard of anything like this before.'

I don't know whether to be reassured or not. Viv kisses me on my cheek.

Viv: 'Whatever is going on, you need to curb your temper.'

Me: 'There is nothing wrong with my temper.'

Viv: 'Three people are dead because of your anger:'

Me: 'I hope you aren't blaming me for that.'

Viv: 'I'm just saying that you need to be very careful how you react to things that you don't like.'

Me: 'So you're telling me not to stick up for my beliefs?'

Viv: 'I'm saying that, for whatever reason, people are being killed when you argue with them. Something weird has been going on ever since you found that hand, and you need to bear that in mind.'

I sigh in frustration. Viv is right, of course; I have to watch my mouth, but that is difficult when the world is full of arseholes. It won't be easy.

Viv: 'I know a good therapist who could help with your anger issues; she helped me when ..."

Me: 'I don't need that shit.'

Viv: 'Then more people will die.'

Me: 'Oh, fuck off.'

Viv sighed heavily, collected her stuff and left, slamming the door hard behind her. I had pissed her off. Fuck, what have I done? Have I just sentenced the woman I love to death?

I tried phoning her, but she wasn't answering; I can't blame her really. I hardly got any sleep that night, I was so worried that she would be visited by "the hand." I was supposed to return to work this morning, with my week's suspension over, but couldn't face it right now. I tried ringing Viv as soon as it was light, but still got no answer. I was just about to drive to Portland, to her flat in Easton, when two middle-aged men in dark blue suits banged on my door, claiming to be government agents.

'Wayne King?' they asked when I opened the door.

'That's me,' I replied. 'How may I help?'

I reluctantly let them into my flat and took them to the kitchen. They told me that they have been made aware that I found a hand in my garden, and that everyone I have got angry with is now dead. They asked to take the hand away for examination, and admitted that the police should have taken it away in the first place. They got quite agitated when I told them the hand had disappeared. The two men, who I noticed smelled of lavender, looked perplexed for a moment, then came straight out and asked me if I had used the hand to hex anyone.

'Of course not,' I replied. Then they asked if I had tried to hex anyone indirectly, from a picture or the television. I told them I had not even thought about it, that I was not a hexer, or anything like that.

'You realise you are dangerous when you lose your temper?' one of the men said. I replied that I was looking at treatment for that, and it would not be a problem. I began to get worried that they knew much more than they were letting on. They told me that if I was seen as a threat to the British government, it was an easy task for them to make me disappear.

'Are you threatening me?' I growled back at them.

'Of course not, we were just saying. The government moves in mysterious ways.' they informed me. One of the men took a large brown envelope from his briefcase and handed it to me.

'Inside are photographs of evil individuals who we would like "gone." They are people who are a danger to the law-abiding citizens of our country, terrorists who threaten the lives of many innocent men, women, and children for their own gain. The world would be a better place without them in it.'

I took the envelope and put it on the table, wondering what these two men actually want of me. Was I being recruited as a government assassin? It feels as if I have woken up in an alternative reality, a surreal world where nothing made sense.

'Think about it,' one of the men said.

'We will be watching you, and if you tell anyone of our meeting ... well, you will be putting their lives in danger too.' I was too stunned to answer back, or question what they had just said, before they bid me a good day and left.

This last week has been like a bad dream, only it was not a dream—it was real. Then I remembered Viv; she would be at work by now if she were still alive. I called her on her mobile, but still got no answer, and I was just about to call her work to check whether she was there or not, when she phoned me. I was relieved, believe you me. Viv told me she had just wanted me to sweat a little and consider the consequences of my anger. As soon as she had got home last night, Vivienne had made a large pentagram on her living-room floor, placed a white candle at each of the five points, cleansed the area with sage, and slept the night in a sleeping bag in the circle, just in case.

'Thank god,' I screamed.

'God has nothing to do with it,' Viv laughed. 'The goddess was looking after me, as she always does.'

'Can I see you tonight?' I asked, hopefully.

'I was hoping you would say that,' Viv replied. 'You can help me clean up the salt I used for the pentagram, and I will cook you your favourite food: bangers and mash, peas and my home-made gravy. You can bring the wine.'

It was an offer I could not refuse.

'See you around seven,' Viv ordered. 'Love you.'

'Love you too.'

To say that I was relieved that Vivienne was ok would be an understatement, and what was I to make of this morning's visitors? I was curious, and opened the package they left, and emptied it out onto the kitchen table. It contained twelve colour portrait photos of men and women of all ages, from around twenty-five to about eighty. I spread them out on the table. There was nothing extraordinary-looking about any of them, that marked them out as evil. They were just regular-looking, casual, smiling people, but then again, what does evil look like? It is the actions that make people evil, not their looks, and I would have to trust what the two government agents told me this morning as "fact." Why would they lie? Then again, why would they threaten to make me disappear if I did not go along with their plans? They made a "request" that I was sure could not possibly work, and anyway, how would I know that it had? If it did work, would I become some kind of assassin for them, to rid the world of evil? I will talk it over with Viv, tonight, maybe. Do I really want her involved? Will I put her life in danger too if I revealed my situation to her? My head began to swim.

Anyway, I have some time to think it over. For now, I decided I would just focus on one of the photos, so I picked one out who I thought looked the most "evil": an old white-haired man, with a long goatee, in his sixties. He had tattoos all up his arms and reminded me a bit of the 70s TV character Catweazle, a necromancer from the time of the Normans, who was cast into the future of 1970s by his bungling magic. I always found him a bit creepy.

What was it the government agent said? Evil individuals who wish to harm innocent people with their actions. I am not expecting anything to happen anyway, but I focused my mind into imagining the Catweazle look-alike in the photo as a bully, a wife-beater, so I could get angry with him. After about five minutes of shouting abuse at him, and hating this person to the core, I needed to calm myself down with a coffee and a roll-up before I did myself an injury. I couldn't believe how angry I could get over an anonymous man in a photograph. When I saw Viv in the evening, I told her about the whole experience. She thought I was daft, and that the whole idea of getting angry at photographs of people was just crazy. She told me to just burn the photos and ignore the threats of my two visitors from this morning.

*

I got up early the next morning and made Viv a cup of tea in bed, then switched the telly on to watch the news. The cost of living going up, energy prices on the rise, Tory in-fighting, and the war in Ukraine escalating. The world has gone crazy! Then the murder, last night, of a prominent environmentalist was announced' "Strangled in his bed," the report said. It was the man I nicknamed Catweazle, from the photograph that I "cursed" yesterday. Shit, fuck me. What is going on? What have I done? The man, the report said, was sixty-three-year-old James Irving, an outspoken activist, who constantly protested against the government departments and big businesses who allow, and indulge in, the destruction and pollution of the environment. I began to curse myself for being so stupid and so gullible, just loud enough for Viv to become concerned. I told her the news about the environmentalist: that the man in the photo I got angry with, had been found strangled in his bed. Vivienne calmed me down, telling me it was just a coincidence and not to be worked up by it, but I wasn't convinced. Something strange was definitely going on, ever since I found that bloody hand.

I felt sick as I drove home, back to Wyke Regis, across the causeway when Viv went to work. I decided that I would burn the other photographs as soon as I got in and try to put the whole thing out of my mind. I got myself into a right tizzy, worrying about it, and got very angry with myself again, to the point where I was cursing myself in front of the bathroom mirror. God, I was so angry with myself that I punched the wall.

By the evening, I had calmed down some, but I was still angry with the two officials who visited me yesterday, so I decided to give the bastards a taste of their own medicine. Then I got angry with the government, and not just ours, because all the governments around the world deserved my wrath. I felt that the whole world was going crazy; with all the wars, the famines, pestilence, and death everywhere, the four horses of the apocalypse were now galloping across the planet.

To tell you the truth, I am angry with everyone in the world right now; every living soul has a part to play in the chaos I am surrounded by, and it is getting worse by the day. I took a deep breath before my mind exploded. Ever since I found the severed hand, my life has just been mad. I need to take some deep breaths and calm down; it was not a good idea to go to sleep in such a foul mood. Hopefully, I will feel better in the morning. Good night.

POSTSCRIPT

A thirty-five-year-old Weymouth man, Wayne King, was found dead in his bed this morning, by his girlfriend, Vivienne Fey. The police revealed that Mr King had been strangled. They are refusing to confirm that a severed hand, of an unknown origin, was found on the deceased's pillow, but Miss Fey has told us that this is true. Our condolences go out to Mr King's family and friends at this sad time.

Wyke Herald, afternoon edition, February 2nd, 2023.

WILLIAM
Kate Knight

I still have his blood under my nails. No matter how hard I scrub, the damn stuff is still there to remind me. The police wouldn't have done a damn thing. They'd have said:
"We need more evidence, sir."
Or
"We are waiting for the CCTV footage, sir."
He'd have been long gone by the time those results appeared. He knew—he knew that I was after him, that is why he was hiding in the dark. He didn't count on me finding him though, did he?

Steph is not my biological child, but I've been in her life from the beginning. We have had our moments, but I see her as my daughter, and always have. I was there when she said her first word, when she took her first steps, and when she laughed for the first time. I was the one who made her brush her teeth and made sure her hair was combed. She knew that I loved her just as much as I loved her mother. Her own father walked out on her mum as soon as she told him that she was expecting. Fucking waster if you ask me. She has never met him nor ever wanted to. She had me as her dad.

The doctors told her mum that she would be okay; they put her in a coma while her brain heals. That's the best place she can be right now. At least while she is asleep, she isn't in any pain.

My wife's screaming that night, when Steph flatlined, is a sound I will never forget, not for as long as I live.

When I heard that she was stable and out of danger, I had to leave the hospital. My wife was at Steph's bedside, holding her hand. Her head was heavily bandaged and she still wore a neck brace, but they said that she should recover. I told my wife that I was going to find him, because he'd scarpered as soon as we arrived. Usually she'd beg me not to, or say that he wasn't worth it, but this time she just told me to be careful. She wanted him dead, the same as I did. No one does that to our girl. No one.

I went straight to The King's Arms, which is where he drinks. He's usually in the corner by the toilets, leching at women and hoping to grope some poor girl who was too drunk to notice. He's had a fair amount of slaps and a few rollockings from angry boyfriends. He won't get barred though, because he's Chris's younger brother. Chris is the owner of the pub, and he makes up the excuse that his brother has special needs. He's special alright, specially dead, and his blood is on my hands. Anyway, he wasn't there so I went to his place, off Gravel Park; the small, white house with the nicotine-brown windows. I bashed on the door several times until his old mum opened it. Surprised me a bit, I thought the old bag had died years ago. She certainly walked like the dead, because it must have taken her a good twenty minutes to get to the door. He wasn't home, but I was smart and told her that I needed him because Chris wanted him to help lock up. That's when she mentioned the old allotment, down behind the station. She said he went there when he wanted time alone. Perfect, I thought. I went straight there and, as I got to the gate, I saw him on his knees crying like a baby. I grabbed a shovel from up against one of the sheds and crept up behind him. He didn't even have a chance to look around before I wrapped the shovel across his head. It knocked him out and he fell into the mud. As I thought of the state of poor Steph, anger took over my mind and my hands. Again and again, I dug that blade into his head and neck, until his head rolled off the mud and onto the grass. I threw down the shovel, and scooped up his head and held it in front of me, as the blood poured out of it. I have never seen a dead man before, so I was curious. His eyes were still twitching, and his tongue went in and out for a while, like he was trying to breathe.

"You won't touch up any more girls now, will ya? Pervert!" I expect they were the last words he heard before he properly died. It was pitch black in the allotment, apart from the light from the half-moon. No one was watching, so I dug up the radishes and buried him where he lay. I put his head between his legs to teach him one final lesson.

I went straight back to my place afterwards to have a shower, and get rid of my clothes and shoes; they were all covered with blood. The water ran red. It was in my hair more than anything. I'm a builder by trade, so my hands are rough. That's why I can't seem to get all the dirt off my hands or the blood from my nails; I expect it will still be there long after I'm gone. I got dressed and went back to the hospital, where my wife still held onto Steph's hand. She looked straight at me, with eyes that were red from crying, when I walked in.

"Well? Did you find him?" I nodded. My wife sighed.

"How is she doing?" I asked.

"No change really. Doctor said they will try and wake her in a day or two, to see if she has had any damage to her brain. They are scanning her again in the morning, to see if there is any improvement. If the swelling hasn't reduced by then, they said they might have to operate. What did he say when you found him?"

I pulled up a chair next to her, so we could chat quietly.

"That wanker didn't say a word. I didn't give him time to. Let's just say that he won't be pushing any more women in front of the night bus when they say 'no'."

My wife frowned at me, like she didn't have a clue what I was saying. "What have you done, Mark?"

She looked concerned. I thought she was worried that I'd get caught, so I reassured her that it was sorted. No one saw me do it.

"Do what Mark? What did you do?"

I stood up and backed away from her. I couldn't understand why she was acting so angrily. "Mark. Tell me. Tell me now, what the fuck you have done to William!"

"I did him in, babe. Buried the prick in the allotment. No one saw me do it. It was pitch black." My wife began screaming like a crazy person; she started punching my chest and crying.

"I wasn't him, Mark, you fucking idiot. He was trying to help her. I wanted to find him to make sure he was alright. Don't you understand? They were friends from school!"

My wife ran from the room and collapsed by the front desk.

"Call the police. My husband has just murdered a man. Please call the police."

I stood by the door in total shock. How could she do that to me? How could she hand me over to the police so willingly? I couldn't move. I wanted to run, but my feet were glued to the spot. A few moments later, two security guys appeared, led me away from my family and cuffed me to a railing until the police arrived.

I was taken to the police station and thrown in a cell. The officers couldn't even look at me. When I asked for a drink they spat in my face and called me scum. The next day I discovered the truth and, as the story unfolded, my brain felt like it was about to implode.

Steph and William had been in the same class at school; Steph had a nurturing nature and befriended him. William had Down Syndrome but, despite his health concerns, was happy in a mainstream school. Steph knew I wouldn't approve of their friendship, so she didn't tell me. The night of the accident, Steph had been drinking with some of her girlfriends and decided to drop in on William on the way home. He always liked to walk her home after a night out, to make sure she got back safely. Chris explained that she stumbled into the bar, giggling and screaming William's name. Chris thought nothing of it and sent William off to take her home.

William spent his evenings in the bar with his brother, because his ageing, disabled mother had trouble caring for his needs. William loved hearing about Steph's adventures from her nights out and was always rewarded by a kiss on the cheek. That was something that William always looked forward to receiving as he had always felt deep love for Steph. That night, the pair were seen on CCTV walking along the path by Gravel Park. William was holding Steph close while she was crying. As the night bus passed, Steph pushed William away, kissed him on the cheek, and ran out into the road. The bus driver slammed on his brakes but collided with Steph, throwing her sideways. Her head connected with the curb, and she was knocked unconscious. It was William who stayed with her in the road, yelling for help while keeping her still and applying pressure to her gushing head wound. William had saved her life. I had murdered the man who saved my daughter's life. I had murdered a nineteen-year-old young man with Downs, whose only sin was wanting my sweet daughter's kiss. He was not a pervert as I had suspected, but a man that showed curiosity for the female form, void of any sexual thoughts. I had murdered a brother, a son, an innocent man, and my daughter's friend. I was the monster, not him. I have asked myself why she hadn't told me about her friendship with William, but I know the answer. Many times, I would come home from work complaining about those who find my comments offensive. I have never been one to hold back a thought. 'Word vomit', my wife calls it.

    William's body was found swiftly, and plagued with guilt I accepted my fate, and confessed to the murder. I am now here, alone in my cell. My bed sheet noose is tied and my chair stands below, waiting for me to kick it away. Steph woke up, thankfully without any permanent damage thanks to William, but she now hates me and I don't blame her one bit. My wife came to see me with the divorce papers; she said the solicitor will see it goes through quickly. I have nothing left now except for the guilt that eats me inside every day.

*

To my wife,

We have been married for nearly 19 years now and, no matter what, I love you more than ever. I know those words must be difficult to hear, but under this monster is still a man who only did what he thought was right at the time. You and Steph are my world, and my anger stopped me from seeing the truth. I wish I could take it back. I miss you both so much. I am doing this because I cannot live with what I have done. I cannot look at myself in the mirror, knowing that the person who stares back at me did those awful things. I hate myself with a deep passion.
Will love you always.

*

To my daughter Steph,

I know you can't and won't forgive me, and I don't deserve to be forgiven. All I can say is that I love you, and if I could take it back, I would. Sorry for being such an arsehole that you felt you couldn't talk to me. Sorry that I took away your friend. I will always love you.

Dad.

*

To my Dad,

We spread your ashes today, after keeping you in the garage for over a year. We took them to the beach at night when the stars were bright. I thought I'd feel angry forever, but I cried when I saw what was left of you dissolved in the waves. I didn't have a chance to tell you, but the reason why I jumped in front of that bus was because so many things were piling up on me. My college exams, my work, you and mum arguing all the time, and because I fell in love with a girl and I know that you would never approve. She ended our relationship because I didn't have the courage to come out and tell you the truth. William was the only normal, stable part of my life, and I loved him like a brother. He has always been sweet and caring, and so full of joy. When we told his mum that he had been murdered, she had a heart attack and died two days later. Chris has disappeared completely: he just cleared out his bank account and left. No one knows where he is, or if he is alright.

Mum said that you were trying to get revenge that night. You didn't even ask about the facts, just jumped to conclusions. William was cremated along with his mother; we used your savings to cover the funerals, we thought it was the least you could do. I always have William with me, because some of his ashes are in a vial I wear in a necklace. I will miss him so much.

Now you have gone, I feel that I need to write this note, even though you will never see it. My therapist said it would help. Mum isn't coping well: she drinks a lot. She says it makes her feel better when she is drunk. I moved out last week, as I can't live with her any more. I still visit most days, if only to check that she is still alive. I have moved into a nice little flat with Joanne. After the accident, I came out to Mum; she was happy for me, where I know you would have hated it. I know that you hated anyone who wasn't like you. Joanne is amazing and treats me like I deserve to be treated, and I return that love to her.

So, Dad, what you did that night caused more than just William's death: many people were affected. Chris is Christ knows where, Mum is slowly killing herself, and William's mum died literally of a broken heart. I had to move on, though; I had to continue to live. I got a second chance that night, thanks to William and I plan to honour him by living it the best way I can. Mum gave me your motor bikes, so I sold them to the bloke down at the showroom. Me and Jo are planning to use the money on a round the world trip. I just hope Mum can cope when we're away.

A memorial plaque was unveiled at the weekend, on the spot where you killed William. The locals donated, and your money went towards it too. It's a huge marble statue of a bumble bee, because William loved watching them buzzing around the allotment while his dad tended to the vegetables. His dad died there too, a few years before. He had a stroke and collapsed in front of William; that's why he knew how to help me. After his dad passed away, William grew obsessed with first aid. He felt that he could have saved his old dad if he knew how.

I'm sure one day I will feel ready to forgive you, but I just can't bring myself to do that yet. You have left such a trail of destruction, so many lives have been affected by your actions. I hope one day we can all move on. I hope that you have found peace wherever you end up.

From Stephany.

HERE, THERE BE DRAGONS
Defoe Smith

Seven traits swallowed down like sleeping pills,
Dull the senses but accept the thrills.
For here, no good man or woman goes,
Dragons are nothing compared to life's illicit passionate throes.

Smother me in succulent delight,
The more the merrier with the sauce of contrite.
One more thing may make the experience sweeter,
Copious amounts of holy wine a banquet for this humble creature.

As I wallow draped in finery with conceited display,
A hunger for flesh from another's silver tray.
Ignore the signposts, it isn't what they meant,
Here there be dragons writhing in seductive content.

Beyond what we know lays the fountain for the youth,
It isn't what we've done that keeps the world at bay from truth.

And after seven deadly sins, what on earth do you think is left?
Questions ... answers ... and death.

Printed in Great Britain
by Amazon